CALLED TO DUTY
BOOK 3 – THE SHIPPING PROBLEM

Doug Murray

CALLED TO DUTY
BOOK 3 – THE SHIPPING PROBLEM

DOUBLE DRAGON

CHAPTER ONE

"Where's your younger half?" Mary Max asked as Frank stepped into her office.

"He's in school, Ma'am." Frank Farrell grinned. "Final exam today."

"Really?" She arched an eyebrow. "What subject?"

"HALO." Frank told her. "Jumping out of an airplane."

"Why in God's name is he doing that?"

"He felt the need," Farrell shrugged. "And, to be honest, it could come in handy down the line."

"Alright," she shook her head. "When do you expect him back?"

"Sometime tomorrow."

"Call me when he gets in," she put a hand on the back of her neck, pressing hard to relieve the tension there. "I need to get you guys working on this one."

"Which one is that?"

"I'd rather wait until you're both in the room." She picked up a folder and began to study the contents, dismissing Frank.

Must be important, he thought as he closed her office door. *I should call Sean and tell him.* He pulled out his cell phone—then stopped. *No,* he told himself. *It'll wait until tomorrow morning.* He nodded once. *Best not to bother him until after his jump.*

Farrell pushed the phone back into his pocket and headed for his office, wondering where the youngster was right now...

Sean Piper was, in fact, some two thousand miles away busily humping his way toward a C 130 sitting on the very edge of the flight line.

"Thought you were going to be late," a young woman in coveralls smiled as he reached the plane's ramp.

"Wanted to check my paravane one more time," he answered, smiling back. "Took a little longer than I expected."

"Did you check your barometric trigger? Make sure it's properly calibrated?"

"Yes Ma'am," he gave the girl a casual salute as he reached the top of the ramp. "I also checked my emergency 'chute' and my backup altimeter," he held up his right hand, showing her the device on his wrist. "Did I forget anything?"

"Did you check your life insurance?" She tapped a control on the wall of the aircraft and stepped back as the door began to close. "Just in case."

"I hadn't thought about that," he raised an eyebrow. "Do you lose many trainees?"

"No," she shook her head. "But I always worry about them before a jump."

"You're way too young to be mothering guys like me." He grinned at her. "You should save it for important things."

"What's more important than the lives of guys like you?" She motioned him to one of the aluminum and nylon seats folded against the side wall. "I mean..."

6

Sean wedged himself into one of the seats—the move made far more difficult by the gear he was wearing. "You're worrying right now!" The plane lurched as it began rolling toward the runway. "Sit down and relax—it'll be okay."

The girl nodded and lowered herself into one of the seats—leaving an unoccupied one between them. "Why are you doing this?" She frowned at him as the plane began to speed up. "You're not in the SEAL's."

"Not in the military at all," he shrugged. "But my Dad was in Special Forces and I wanted to get all the training he did."

The plane rocked a bit, then settled as it took to the air.

"Why?"

"Seemed the right thing to do." He shrugged again. "And I might need the training eventually." He looked at his companion. "How about you? Why are you here?"

The girl—her nametag said 'Sobkowiak' but Sean knew her name was 'Connie'--sat back to think about that.

"I..." Her shrug mirrored his. "I didn't want to go to college—no real reason to spend all that money. The Air Force..." She gestured around her. "I love flying and this job gives me the chance to spend a lot of time in the air." She glanced at her watch. "Which reminds me..." She pulled an oxygen mask from her belt and held it up. "Time to go on O2."

"Right," Sean had a small tank attached to his pack and quickly put it on and adjusted the flow."

7

"As I was saying," she smiled at him. "I like to fly—and it gives me the chance to take care of nice young men like you—make sure you are properly prepared for a jump."

Sean smiled back. 'Connie' had been the jumpmaster for three of his drops. She'd taken great care to check his gear before each of the drops, making sure that all the lines and straps were where they were supposed to be. Some of those checks had included soft touches in rather intimate spots—and Sean wasn't sure if those meant anything although he rather hoped they did. He hadn't spent *any* time with a girl since his rather one-sided romance with Angie had crashed and burned.

At least that got me working with Farrell, he thought. *And got my Mother and Sister taken care of!*

Sean still hoped to have normal relationships now and then—and he liked Connie. She was pretty in a fresh-faced and earnest kind of way and a quick and completely illegal check of her record had shown him that she was honest and, in the opinion of her commanders, completely trustworthy.

Now all he had to do was find a way to ask her out...

"We'll be at the target height in just over five minutes," she told him. "Time to get into position."

Sean nodded and pushed himself onto his feet. He made his way to the edge of the closed ramp where he stopped while Connie checked his rigging.

"Why are you here?" She asked him as she checked the security of his straps. "I mean, really?"

8

"They weren't doing any HALO jumps at Banning," he told her as she pulled one of his shoulder straps tighter. "So I used a work contact to get a couple of rides here at Hurlburt Field."

"How did you know that we do jumps here?"

"Your planes are kept ready for SEAL Team tasking and I know just how often the guys in the teams like to practice..."

"Okay," she gave his gear one final look then stepped back. "But why do a solo jump? Why not wait for some of the others?"

"Have to get back to the office," he grinned. "Can't let them think they can get along without me."

"Oh," she frowned. "Does that mean..."

The door suddenly *CLANKED* loudly and began to open.

"Grab a safety line!" Sean yelled. "Quick!"

It was too late. Caught by surprise Connie was pulled backwards by the rush of air...

Right out the back of the aircraft.

"Shit!" Sean muttered as he raced down the ramp and dove after her.

CHAPTER TWO

High-altitude military parachuting is a method of delivering military personnel and military supplies from an aircraft out of sight and out of reach of most equipment. A HALO (High Altitude Low Open) jump demands that the parachutist free falls for a period of time.

Free-fall has been practiced by civilian skydivers since the 1960's although seldom from the kind of altitude used by Military personnel who routinely jump from altitudes of between fifteen and thirty-five thousand feet.

Sean had planned his jump from twenty-five thousand feet and had hoped to do it at night, a request denied by the base commander...

Which is a good thing, he thought as he pulled his arms tightly to his side to increase his speed. *Or I wouldn't be able to see her!*

As it was, he could just make out Connie below—she had spread out in a stable position, slowing her fall and making it possible for him to catch up.

He hoped.

Just keep straight, he told himself, and let yourself catch up. He took a deep breath. *The hard part will begin then!*

He thought about what he would need to do.

I'm going to have to get the best grip on her I can, he knew. *It would help if she was conscious*. He could see that she still had her oxygen bottle. *If she is, she can wrap herself around me...*

A small part of his brain told him that might be fun.

No time for that now, he risked a glance at his altimeter. *Twenty-two thousand feet...* He did some math in his head. *I'll have to get to her before we reach ten thousand or we might not have time to get our act together...* He tried to judge his speed—an impossibility with no frame of reference. *Just keep going and hope for the best...*

He inched closer, closer...

Can't hit her too hard, he told himself. *Gotta match velocity as nearly as I can...*

He opened his position a little, reducing his speed just enough—he hoped...

He was within twenty feet...Ten...Five...

He grabbed one of her arms, putting the two of them into a spin for a moment while he pulled her closer together.

"Grab me!" He shouted into the slipstream. "Wrap your legs around me!"

He could see her face now—white with cold and fear—but her eyes were steady and she nodded once before wrapping her arms around his chest before pulling herself closer and repeating the action with her legs.

He closed his own arms around her and, for a few seconds, concentrated on stabilizing their fall. If he couldn't do that, the paravane lines might become snarled and keep the canopy from opening.

She kept still, not interfering as he worked, not wanting to break his concentration.

"Okay," he said into her ear. "I'm going to open the chute in three..." He tightened his grip with his left arm while grabbing the chute release in his right hand. "Two..." He swallowed once, then: "One!"

He pulled hard on the release...

***

During a typical HALO exercise, a jumper will reach terminal velocity within about 60 seconds (depending on wind and his body position). That meant that as the paravane deployed, Sean and Connie were subjected to around three 'G's of force which meant that Connie's One hundred twenty pounds instantly became a three hundred sixty pound weight dragging at her grip. For a long moment, she held on with a desperate force—matched by Sean's.

And then they were floating downward, supported by the fully-opened paravane.

"You all right?" Sean asked in the suddenly quiet air.

"I think so," Connie looked into his eyes. "You saved my life!"

"We still have to get down," Sean looked at the landscape below. "We're well short of the drop zone—all I can see down there is scrub and sand."

"Do whatever you can," she took a deep breath. "Drop me if you have to."

"Not a chance of that," Sean smiled. "Just hold on tight..."

A moment later, they were down. At the last minute Sean had found a small clearing and by 'gulling' out the paravane, he'd been able to put them down in it—not as gracefully as he would

12

have liked, but softly enough that neither of them were hurt.

"Okay," he said a moment later as they slid to a halt—her on top. "You can let go now."

"Just a minute." She pulled him closer and kissed him hard. "That's for saving me." She kissed him again. "And that's for getting the two of us down in one piece."

"Any time, Ma'am." Sean grinned as the two of them disengaged and sat across from one another for a long second. "Just one thing."

"Yes?"

"When I get back down here," he raised an eyebrow. "Would you go out to dinner with me?"

She looked at him for a long moment, then leaned forward and kissed him again, her arms going around him. "Anytime, Mr. Piper. Anytime at all!"

***

"You look like you had a good time," Frank Farrell gave his partner an up-and-down glance. "A very good time!" He shook his head. "I thought parachuting was supposed to be hard work."

"Hard enough," Sean paced the older man as they made their way through the crowd at Reagan airport. "What's going on?"

"Mary Max has something for us," Farrell dodged an overweight tourist's backpack. "Says she won't go over it until we're both there."

"Important?"

"If it was vital, she'd have asked me to call you back immediately." He pushed open the door that led to the parking garage. "I figure it's something on the back burner that involves computers in one way or another."

"Russian hackers!" Sean smiled. "Gotta be—what else is going on that would need our attention?"

"You might be right," Farrell led the way to his car—an unassuming Gray Lexus parked in the lot reserved for members of Congress and VIP's. "In any case, we'll find out soon enough." He looked at his watch. "Mary Max is waiting for us."

"Now?" Sean tossed his bag into the car's trunk. "I don't even get to shower and change?"

"She said to bring you there ASAP," Farrell shrugged. "That means now."

Sean sighed as the car left the garage and headed for the 14th Street Bridge, thankful that the traffic wasn't too heavy yet.

***

Traffic was, in fact, light enough that Farrell pulled into the FBI Building's garage only twenty minutes later.

"Not bad for a five-minute drive!" He told Sean, smiling. "One of these days, somebody will put in a Ferry and really speed things up!"

"It'd be easier just to concrete the river over," the younger man stepped out and straightened his short-sleeved shirt. "I'm really under-dressed for this. Are you sure..."

"You wouldn't have worried about that a year ago." Farrell grinned. "Don't tell me you're growing up!"

14

"It's not that, it's just..."

"Mary Max will understand." Farrell reached the elevator first, pressed the button for the appropriate floor. "She's good that way."

Sean sighed again—then resigned himself to the meeting and followed his partner down the long corridor and across to the small meeting room where Mary Max was waiting.

"Gentlemen," she nodded as the two entered. "Please be seated."

Mary Max Halston had been a fixture in the intelligence services for more than twenty years. Like many old-timers, she knew where a great number of bodies were buried and that knowledge, coupled with her undeniable capability, had given her no small amount of power--and a great deal of independence.

She was going to test just how far that independence went now.

"You've both heard about the Russians 'hacking' the recent election and about the 'collusion' between them and the new administration?"

"Impossible not to," Sean nodded. "If you pay any attention to the news at all."

"Well," Mary Max produced two folders and slid them across the table. "Here is the complete file on the incident."

"But," Sean looked up after a quick scan of the file. "There's nothing here! No proof at all—nothing but opinions..."

"They call it 'Consensus'." She shook her head. "Consensus..."

"Just like Global Warming." Frank put the folder down on the table. "So they agree that something happened but don't know what." He looked at his boss. "What do you want us to do?"

"I want you to look into this—find out whether they really hacked into the DNC and whether anyone in this country was giving them aid of any kind." She looked at the two of them. "Do you think you can do that quickly and quietly?"

"I thought we didn't get into political matters?" Sean tapped the folder. "Judging by this 'proof', this is nothing but."

"Normally," she looked at the young man, "you'd be right—but this is paralyzing half the government and building up to what might turn out to be a real crisis," she shook her head. "I'd like to head it off before that happens."

"We'll need more information than this!" Frank spread his hands. "What kind of authority do I have?"

"The usual." She looked at Sean. "How about you? Can you put the politics aside and dig into this hard enough to find out what's really going on?"

"I can certainly try," He looked at his partner. "But we'll need a lot more than this to do anything!"

"Go to the FBI—check what their 'Cyber CSI' crew has." She frowned. "I assume they have *something* to draw their 'consensus' on."

"I'll get on it first thing in the morning, Ma'am." Sean bit into his lower lip. "If they have anything at all, I'll see what it amounts to."

"Do that," Mary Max pushed her chair back a little, relaxing. "And tell me," she looked at Sean. "Who's the girl?"

"Ma'am?"

"I see just a hint of lipstick on your collar—not to mention a slight relaxation of your usual taut posture." She smiled. "Ergo, you found a girl."

"I don't know if I'd call it that, Ma'am."

"What should I call it?"

"I'm not really sure..." He shrugged and smiled back. "It's possible that I found a girl—but I'm not really sure yet."

"Don't let it interfere with your work."

"I won't, Ma'am."

"Good," she made a shooing motion with her right hand. "Now get out of here and get to work—I'll expect a report in forty-eight hours."

"Two days," Farrell nodded. "Yes Ma'am."

Before the door had even closed, Farrell was looking at his partner and asking: "You found a girl?"

CHAPTER THREE

Sean arrived at the entrance to the FBI's 'Cyber' office early the next morning. He was met by James Tarver, the same supervisor who had accompanied him during his last visit.

"Agent Tarver," Sean smiled at the man. "Good to see you again."

"You too," Tarver returned the smile. "I hear you've moved up in the world."

Sean shrugged. "How so? I'm still working for Mary Max..."

"And take my word for it, that's a very good place to be working," Tarver motioned Sean through the door and into the Cyber division's office. "What can we do for you this time?"

"I've been tasked with looking into the Russian hacks into the election." Sean looked around. "I'd like to see what you have."

"Mary Max got our report."

"The one that talks about a 'consensus'?" Sean frowned. "That's what she wants me to look into—what's behind that 'consensus'? Do you still have the DNC's main computer? I'd like to look at that."

"We didn't take the computer—it was felt that it might appear we were tampering with the election." Tarver's face had gone quite still. "Mr. Comey didn't want to anything that might be construed as questionable."

"Mr. Comey," Sean nodded. "I see. What about the other guy-- Podesta's computer?"

"Nope," Tarver shook his head. "Same thing."

Sean took a deep breath. "What do you have?"

Tarver sighed. "A private organization named CrowdStrike was called in by the Democratic National Committee to analyze the hack against their computer system." He looked at Sean. "Apparently Ms. Clinton didn't trust us and Mr. Comey wasn't willing to make a stink about it." He held up a hand. "I didn't agree but I'm pretty far down the ladder here."

"I understand.'

"We did get a full report of what CrowdStrike eventually found—I've got a copy over here..." He gestured Sean to follow him to his desk.

"As I'm sure you know, attribution of hackers is a very new practice. We—and this CrowdStrike group--rely on the kind of methods that we can identify with a specific hacker—you know, their preferred worms and malware..."

"Is that what 'CrowdStrike did?"

"Apparently. According to their report, CrowdStrike's co-founder, one Dimitri Alperovitch, found coding signatures that pointed to two separate groups of Russians he calls Cozy Bear and Fancy Bear." He sighed. "Cozy Bear uses a tool called SeaDaddy to exfiltrate information from the DNC computer—the same tool, or one so incredibly similar as to be identical, was previously identified by Symantec (the Virus Protection People) as belonging to a group of Russian hackers known to operate at the behest of Russia's FSB, their main intelligence agency."

"Is that all they had?" Sean asked.

"CrowdStrike also found that another group of hackers--*Fancy Bear*-- was sending command and control instructions from a server with an Internet Protocol (IP) address of 176.31.112.10. This was the same IP address linked to an attack against the German parliament in 2015." Tarver shook his head. "The DNC attacker used an identical command and control server." He looked at Sean. "That wasn't all from 'CrowdStrike'--Microsoft also identified the communication program as one that belonged to Fancy Bear, who Microsoft had, at the time, identified as "Strontium'."

Tarver sat down, gesturing Sean to do the same. "As you know, one of the elements of a truly advanced hack is that it opens, and keeps open, a communication channel with the hacked network which allows the hacker to avoid detection while he continues to find and take information in all parts of the hacked network. The DNC hack used software that is known to be used by Fancy Bear." He looked at Sean. "The Dems called in other firms and they all found similar evidence."

"That's it?" Sean frowned. "You didn't examine *anything* and your evidence is a bunch of guesswork from a couple of private firms?"

"I admit that this kind of open source evidence isn't conclusive--but it's all we've got."

"I thought the President—Mr. Obama—asked you guys to review this whole thing?"

"He did but without seizing the hardware there wasn't much else we could do..."

"I guess not." Sean stood up. "Mind if I keep this report?"

"Take it with my blessing." Tarver smiled at him. "And if you find anything more, could you please keep me in the loop?" He shook his head. "Nobody else seems interested in doing that."

"I'll try," Sean shook the man's hand once again. "Although I can't promise..."

***

"So that's the story," Sean reported to Mary Max later that day. "The DNC didn't trust the FBI to investigate the hacking so they let an outside agency come in and look around." He shook his head. "Weird as that may sound.'

"You saw the stuff in Podesta's e-mails," Frank put in. "Wanna bet that there's a lot worse in the DNC's backup files?"

"Politics should not come into play here," Mary Max intoned. "The FBI is supposed to be apolitical."

"And it was," Frank frowned. "Until recently."

"Not our problem," Mary Max looked at Sean. "What do you know about..." She glanced at the report he had given her. "Crowdstrike?"

"They're an American cybersecurity technology company, wholly owned by CrowdStrike Holdings, Inc." Sean shrugged. "I haven't had time to look into the holding company yet."

"Understood," Mary Max told him. "Go on."

"Yes Ma'am," Sean referred back to his notes then continued: "The company provides endpoint security, threat intelligence, and incident response services to customers in more than 170 countries. They've recently been called in on both the Sony Pictures and the DNC e-mail hacks."

He looked up from his notes. "Company was co-founded by George Kurtz—a money guy, and Dmitri Alperovitch on whom I have no real information. Shawn Henry, who used to be a senior FBI agent--he led their Cyber Division for a time—now he runs the proactive and incident response services."

"So the Dems went to an ex-FBI agent who's now a gun-for-hire instead of trusting the FBI," Mary Max shook her head. "I love the way these things work!"

"I haven't had time to go into the fine details of their evaluation of the DNC hack..."

"You'll have to go to their headquarters and go through everything they have," Mary Max sighed. "And even then, I suspect they'll do whatever they can to block you." She made a note. "I'll arrange access and see if I can get some pressure put on by my superiors to get you a federal warrant." She looked at Sean. "It'll take a day or two."

"Okay," he nodded slowly. "I'll spend the time looking things over from here and see if there's anything that was missed that might give us a lead..."

"What do you want me to do while Sean is working his side of the street?" Frank asked.

"Stay around here for now—help Sean in any way you can, then, when all the paperwork comes in, go with him to... She looked at Sean. "Where did you say this company was based?"

"California, Ma'am." He smiled. "Irvine, California."

"Irvine, California. Use the time we have to collect whatever equipment you think you'll need."

"Will do, Ma'am."

"Find something we can work with," she looked at the two agents. "This whole thing smells bad! I'm depending on you two to find out why." She made a dismissive gesture. "Now get to work-- I've got people to see."

Farrell stood up, gesturing to Sean to join him. "We'll be waiting."

***

"Where are you going?" Farrell asked as the two headed out the door.

"Our office—my computer is there."

"I'll meet you there in a couple of hours," he hit the elevator button. "There're a few things I have to take care of."

"Meet me at the range," Sean told him. "I need to fire a couple of clips off to keep in practice," he smiled. "I didn't get to do any shooting while I was in Florida."

"The range at five?" Farrell waited for Sean's nod. "Okay, see you there."

They parted as the elevator door opened, Farrell entering to go down to the ground floor while Sean continued down the corridor to the office he shared with the older man.

He was almost there when the alarm went off— the klaxons in the hall bellowing out its two-tone warning over and over and over...

***

"Problem on the Pennsylvania Avenue side!" A security man yelled as he passed Sean. "Some kind of riot!"

Sean frowned for a moment, trying to decide the best thing to do—then he shrugged and ran in the wake of the other man.

He might be needed.

***

Crap! Sean thought a few seconds later as he slid to a stop in the hall just beyond the building's Pennsylvania Avenue lobby. He could see that the area ahead was full of arguing people--some were agents trying to create some kind of order.

But too many were civilians—many carrying signs and banners—were visible—and they were making so much noise that Sean couldn't hear out anything above them and the roar of the crowd.

That didn't really matter. He could see that the security men were beginning to gain some kind of control over the mob—breaking them up, pushing them away from the interior of the building.

They don't need me here, he decided as he watched the melee in front of him. *The Security guys are trained for this sort of thing. I'm just...*

He froze as a familiar face jumped out at him.

That's Mary Max! He took a long step forward, entering the chaos of the lobby. He could see that his boss was trapped in a tiny space between two groups of civilians. One of those groups, led by a tall man with a beard, was pressing close, haranguing her.

I can't leave her in the middle of that! He decided—and began to move forward toward the beleaguered woman.

Now twenty years of age, Sean Piper had just reached his physical maturity. He had his father's height and build—and a lifetime of martial arts practice had made him faster, stronger, and harder than just about any civilian.

These civilians—these protestors—were no match for him.

I don't want to hurt anyone, Sean told himself as he drove into the yelling mob, using his strength and size to push his way through. *Just move them out of the way...*

He'd gone about ten feet before he was forced into a confrontation. An overweight man with a ghostly white pallor (clearly not someone who spent a lot of time outdoors) poked at Sean's chest with the end of a wooden 1x4 that held a sign of some kind.

Sean didn't allow it to touch him, sweeping the attack away with his left hand before breaking the wood with his right. He swept past the overweight man before that worthy even realized what had happened.

The crowd was beginning to realize that they had bitten off more than they could chew as the Security men started to expand their perimeter, forcing the mass back toward the doors. It would take some time but, eventually, they would all be forced back outside.

Sean didn't want to wait. Mary Max was still surrounded by angry men and women and the sooner he got to her, the better.

25

He was more than halfway to her when one of the protestors produced a knife.

The knife wielder was a thin, pale young man who couldn't be any older than Sean—quite unlike some of the tougher-looking individuals who had been quick to get out of his way.

As Sean slid to a halt, the man thrust the knife toward Sean's left side—low enough to hit a kidney and, perhaps, kill him.

Under normal circumstances, Sean would simply have disarmed the young man and moved on—but he was in the middle of an unruly crowd and he didn't want to turn them into an angry mob with the smell of blood in their nostrils. This time he had to disarm his opponent without too much fuss—and quickly before any of the others got ideas.

Sean blocked the thrust with his left forearm and grabbed the man's wrist with his right hand—this gave him enough control that he could ensure there wouldn't be a wild swing of the blade that might hurt one of the people still pressed around him.

A quick twist dropped the knife to the floor and an equally quick open-handed thrust to the chin yielded the sound of teeth shattering.

The young man staggered, half-conscious, and Sean left him wobbling in place—held up by the crowd as much as his own legs.

Mary Max was only a few feet away now and Sean sped up—his right hand closed around the shoulder of one of those pressing up against his boss—and a quick move spun the man out of his way.

"Need a hand, Ma'am?" He said as he reached her side.

"Nice to see you," the older woman smiled. "Do you think you can get me past this bunch?"

"NO!" A very fat woman screamed, holding up a sign that said something about Russia. "YOU HAVE TO DO WHAT WE SAY! YOU WORK FOR US!"

"I don't think so," Sean took the sign away from her. "Now get out of the way—I don't want to hurt anyone."

The woman screamed again—something unintelligible—and pushed a man toward him.

Sean didn't hesitate. He elbowed the man standing on his left to get a little room before sweeping the legs out from beneath the man stumbling toward him.

"Get out of the way, Ma'am." Sean was now facing the screaming woman. "It's time for you to leave."

"I WILL NOT LEAVE!" She shouted into his face. 'THIS IS MY COUNTRY!" She swung wildly at him, flailing away with both hands.

Sean blocked the blows before, unwilling to hurt the woman, he slipped a leg behind her left knee and forced her down until she fell to the floor.

He stepped past her as she lay, still screaming, and escorted Mary Max through the remainder of the crowd that was more than anxious to give him room.

"What is all this about?" He asked.

"They're protesting something," she shook her head. "They don't really know what." She glanced at him. "I'm glad you showed up when you did."

27

They reached the outside door and Sean opened a way past the protestors there, guiding Mary Max out onto the street where he turned one way and led her past the remainder of the crowd.

"Those people are crazy," he frowned as they reached an empty corner. "What are they trying to accomplish?"

"They're being manipulated." Mary Max had her phone out and was dialing quickly. "By elements who want to destabilize the government." She shook her head. "We've got to find out what really happened during the election—it's the only way we can get everyone to calm down."

"I'll get right on it, Ma'am." Sean looked around. "As soon as I know you're safely away from here."

It took only a few minutes before a car—dispatched at Mary Max's call—arrived. Sean opened the door for her and waited until she was safely away before turning back toward the FBI Building.

He decided to bypass the Pennsylvania Avenue entrance and go around to the 'E' Street door.

***

"You're late!" Farrell said as Sean entered the firing range.

"Yeah," he shrugged. "Got hung up by the 'demonstration' at the door."

"Security should have handled that..."

"They did—but I saw Mary Max trapped on one side and I just couldn't leave her there."

"Was she hurt?"

"Angry more than anything," Sean drew his Glock and put it on the firing stand. "What were you up to?"

"Arranging for our flight to California." Farrell smiled. "I was hoping to get one of the company jets but none are available." He looked Sean up and down. "We'll have to fly coach."

Sean shrugged again. "So be it," a smile worked itself onto his face. "Shoot you for the aisle seat!"

"That doesn't seem quite fair..."

"I'll fire at fifty feet—you can bring your target in to twenty-five."

"It's still not fair." Farrell smiled. "But close enough!" He put his weapon next to Sean. "Who goes first!"

CHAPTER FOUR

The next morning it became clear that it didn't matter who won or lost. The flight to Los Angeles was only about 30 percent full and both Sean and Farrell had an entire row to themselves.

Sean used his space and time to do some schoolwork. He only needed another six credit hours to get his degree—something his mother was anxiously waiting for.

He managed to catch up on History and was nearly finished with Math when he had to close down his computer for final approach to LAX.

The terminal was, as usual, jammed. Fortunately, Mary Max had arranged a pick-up by the local FBI office and, after picking up their checked handguns, they were on their way downtown.

Their driver, a sharply-dressed young woman, identified herself as Jennifer Gannon: "I understand you guys are here to look into CrowdStrike Holdings." She pulled a finger drive out of her pocket and handed it to Sean. "This has all the information we've been able to find on them."

"Thanks," Sean pulled out his laptop and inserted the drive. "We can use everything you have."

"There's not much there," Gannon slipped into an empty spot on the freeway, barely missing a gray Leaf as she did so. "Company's been around for a while—local police give them a clean bill of health." She shrugged and hit the gas, ducking into an HOV lane. "I had a look too," she glanced at Sean. "They seem clean."

"Good," Farrell nodded. "We'll head out there first thing tomorrow. I trust your office has arranged transport?"

"They've assigned me to take you wherever you want to go." She slowed as taillights turned red all around her. "If you don't have a problem with that."

"No problem at all," Farrell smiled. "It's always good to have a local available to give us their assessment of the situation."

"Good," Gannon pressed her horn and eased the car past a minor fender bender. "Irvine is about 40 miles from downtown. Traffic," she glanced at Farrell. "Is a bear until about ten..."

"Pick us up at ten." Farrell smiled. "I assume you have a place for us to stay?"

"Yes sir," she hit the horn again, snarling at the driver that tried to cut her off. "We have you booked at the Omni," she smiled. "It's a nice place—you should be comfortable there."

"Good," Farrell stared at the traffic completely blocking the road ahead. "I hope we get there in time to get some sleep."

"It's always like this," Gannon sighed. "Permanent rush hour..."

"Take Sepulveda," Sean put in. "It should be faster."

"You're familiar with the area?"

"My computer is," Sean smiled. "And according to the information it's giving me, Sepulveda is our best bet."

31

"Sepulveda it is," she smashed a first down on the horn again. "Although it might take a few minutes to get off the freeway..."

***

Gannon dropped the two off at the Omni and, after a quiet meal in the hotel restaurant, Sean and Frank retreated to their rooms. The three hour time change made ten PM local time feel like one in the morning so it was really easy to slip into bed.

As they slept, a computer security seminar started in Paris, France...

***

"All right, Ladies and Gentleman." The speaker, a Mr. Radcliffe, looked around the smallish ballroom. "It has been decided that we will break up into smaller groups for the day—each of you has been told to which room you are to go—we will meet again after lunch to discuss whatever you come up with and make plans for this afternoon's meetings." He smiled. "There are refreshments in each room so..." He made a shooing motion. "Please go where you have been assigned."

The men and women looked at the printed page each had been given and, slowly, began to file out of the ballroom. There was some confusion in the halls but, eventually, all found their assigned spot and began discussing some aspect of the current hacking crisis.

One team, led by John Torrico, were discussing developments in the US and French elections when a well-dressed man stepped through the door.

"John Torrico?" He asked, holding a photo in his hand and looking from face to face.

"I'm Torrico," the man standing in the front of the room said.

"So you are," the man in the doorway smiled and produced a handgun with a long suppressor. He swung it up and fired three times, each shot hitting Torrico in the center of mass.

"Thank you all for your courtesy," the pistol disappeared. "Good day."

He exited while the people in the room sat, frozen, in their assigned seats.

***

"Did our warrant come in?" Sean asked his partner as they met in the hotel restaurant for breakfast early the next morning.

"Nope." Frank shook his head. "Mary Max says it'll take a while."

"So just what do we do?"

"We'll go out and talk to the people at Crowdstrike." Farrell shrugged. "Maybe they'll give us what we want without any problems."

"I doubt that," Sean pulled a metallic object from his pocket. "I'm glad I brought this along."

"What is it?"

Sean placed the object—a metal and plastic rectangle about four inches long and one wide on the table between them. "I used to use this when I was in High School." He bit his lip. "It's a kind of

33

siphon—if I place it in close contact with a computer hard drive or near a Wi-Fi server, it'll download all the information it can reach." Sean grinned. "It's got a neat little program that does a nice job of bypassing low-level security—like passwords and the like."

Farrell peered at the device for a moment. "This can't be legal."

"Of course not," Sean picked the device up and put it in a pocket. "And nothing I find with it will be usable in a court of law." He raised an eyebrow. "But we're not looking for evidence, right? We just want information."

"Yeah, I guess, but..."

"If you don't want me to use it," Sean shrugged. "I'll keep it in my pocket the whole time."

"That might be better."

"Okay," Sean spread his hands. "We'll just hope they're co-operative." He looked at his partner with as much innocence as he could muster. "I'm sure they will be."

"Shut up and order breakfast," Farrell snarled. "Gannon will be here to pick us up in under an hour."

"Whatever you say, partner." Sean smiled. "Whatever you say..."

***

The drive to Irvine took longer than Sean had expected—nearly two hours through traffic far heavier than he was used to in Washington (although very much like that in New York). He used the time to check e-mail and activate the device in his pocket.

He really didn't think the folks at Crowdstrike were going to be co-operative.

"That's it over there," Gannon told them, nodding to a modern glass-sided cube sitting in the middle of a patch of well-watered grass. "I'll drop you at the entrance and wait in the parking lot."

"Not curious about what they'll say?"

Gannon smiled as she turned into the short driveway. "My boss prefers that our office not be involved," she looked at Farrell. "I'm hoping you'll fill me in on what you find out."

"We'll do that thing." Farrell opened his door and stepped onto the short-paved path that led to the front entrance.

"And I don't think we'll be long," Sean told her as he joined his partner.

Crowdstrike's front door opened automatically as the two men approached. A desk fronted with what looked like a block of malachite stood in the middle of the lobby beyond.

"Can I help you?" A bright young man dressed in a white shirt and red tie sat behind the desk.

"I hope so," Farrell held up his badge. "We've come to discuss the Russian hacking."

"That's Mr. Torrico's area." The young man punched a query into his keyboard. "He's out of the office right now..."

"When will he be back?"

"Not for a few days," the young man treated them to a professional smile. "Will his assistant do?"

"Sure," Farrell shrugged. "I'll be happy to see what she has to say."

"I'll buzz her," the young man gestured to a pair of couches. "If you'll have a seat?"

"She'll tell us nothing," Sean whispered as they sat.

"We'll see." Farrell looked around. "Nice place. Looks really new."

"The whole company is new," Sean raised an eyebrow. "Founded in 2011—this building came about two years later."

"Computer security must be lucrative."

"It is if you're good," Sean smiled wryly. "And discrete."

"Gentlemen." The two looked to their side where an attractive middle-aged woman was emerging from an elevator. "I'm Ingrid Neilson—John Torrico's associate. I'm told you have some questions?"

"Yes, Ma'am." Farrell showed her his credentials. "We're hoping you can supply some answers."

"I'll see what I can do," she gestured for them to follow her. "This way."

The three stepped into the elevator where Ms. Neilson slipped an ID card into a slot before pushing a button. "We can't be too careful," she smiled as the door closed.

Behind them, a well-dressed man stepped into the lobby.

***

"And that's as much as I can show you, Gentlemen." Ms. Nielson gestured to the printouts she had produced from a file in her desk. "We guarantee confidentiality to our clients."

"We'll have a federal warrant in a day or two." Farrell smiled. "Do you really want us to serve it?"

"If you get a warrant I will, of course, give you all the information I have." She smiled. "But I'll be surprised if any judge grants your request."

"Why?"

Mr. Nielson looked at Sean. "United States law gives a great deal of latitude to companies dealing with sensitive documents. You would need quite a strong argument to allow you to violate our guarantee of confidentiality."

"There is the question of National Security."

"I see nothing here that would impact that security." She shrugged. "Of course, others might have a different view." She looked at her visitors. "Let's see if that's the case, shall we?" She stood up. "Come back when you have your warrant."

"We will, and..."

The door opened and a dark-skinned man in a light-colored suit stepped into the doorway, looking from face to face until his gaze lit on Ms. Nielson at which time he pulled something out of his pocket, looked at it, and smiled: "Ms. Ingrid Nielson?" He asked.

"Yes." She looked at him. "What can I do for you?"

The man smiled and smoothly drew a pistol with a long sound-suppressor from beneath his jacket. "You can die."

He brought the pistol smoothly into firing position...

38

CHAPTER FIVE

Sean and Farrell went into action at the same instant--Farrell reached for the Glock which was holstered in a shoulder rig under his jacket. He knew that he couldn't possibly draw it before the man in the doorway fired...

But he had to try!

Sean also realized that he wouldn't have time to draw his own pistol—so he did something desperate. He hurled the metal and plastic ballpoint with which he'd been taking notes toward the assailant's eyes, spinning it like a football as it left his fingers.

In almost the same motion, he dove toward the frozen woman behind the desk, trusting his partner to cover him—even though he didn't think either one of them had a chance to act in time...

Sean hung in a pocket of time, bracing for the bullets that were going to hit him in the back any second now...

No bullets came and Sean drove into Ms. Nielson, carrying her down and behind the desk just as Farrell's gun came clear. He could see the result of Sean's effort—the young agent's pen had flown faster and straighter than either of them could have imagined. Hitting the gunman in the face, the point penetrating his skin just an inch or so below his left eye.

The man had reacted involuntarily, flinching at the impact so close to his eye...

39

He never had time to recover before Farrell put three shots into his center of mass dropping him to the floor.

"You okay, Sean?" Farrell asked as he kicked the assailant's gun to one side. "Helluva throw!"

"I'm fine," Sean pushed himself to his feet and reached down to help Ms. Nielson into her chair. "How about you, Ms. Nielson?"

"I'm..." She looked at the young man who was now leaning against her desk, his eyes full of concern. "You saved my life..."

"Any idea who this was?" Farrell asked the bright young woman as he searched the gunman's clothing for some kind of ID.

"I've never seen him before," She shook her head. "Why did he try to kill me?" She hugged herself, suddenly shivering. "I haven't done anything..."

"Ms. Nielson!" The bright young man from the lobby rushed into the office. "Mr. Torrico is dead! Shot! We just got a message"

"Your partner's dead and <u>this</u> man came here after you," Farrell nodded at the body on the floor. "He had your picture," he held up a photo he'd taken from the man's pocket. "And he verified your identity before he drew his weapon." Farrell picked up the suppressed handgun.

"These men just saved my life." Ms. Nielson took a deep breath. "What were you saying about John?"

"Someone walked into the conference, asked for him by name, and shot him when he identified himself."

40

"Interesting," Farrell nodded. "Sane thing almost happened here..."

"Crap!" Sean bit his lip and pulled out his cell phone. "Gannon!" He almost shouted as the agent answered. "Has another car pulled in since we arrived?"

"Two have," she answered. "One stayed for a few minutes then left, the other..." There was a pause as she looked around. "The other one is still here—parked at the far end of the lot."

"Get the license number and call for back-up. There's been a shooting here and that car could be the shooter's." Sean looked at his partner. "Don't go near it—just call for backup!"

"Will do," Gannon's voice was brisk. "I'm hanging up now..."

The connection was broken.

"You got this, Frank?" Sean asked, coming to his feet.

"I got it..." Farrell nodded. "Go!"

Sean went, running toward the stairs—the elevator would be too slow.

Moments later, he reached the ground floor and sped to the door, sliding to a halt as it opened before him.

Can't appear as if I'm looking for trouble! He realized, slowing himself to a normal walk. *Gotta look like anyone else just coming out of the building...*He took out his phone, dialed Gannon.

"I'm coming out the front door," he told her. "Is our suspect still there?"

"He hasn't moved." The girl's voice was calm, controlled. "I have both local and FBI officers on the way."

41

"Good," Sean stepped out and off the curb. "Now just where..." He looked around, saw the small parking lot to his right. "Okay, I see you." He turned in that direction, doing his best to look inconspicuous. "Which one is our target?"

"White KIA—I think it's a rental. Back right-hand corner of the lot."

"Okay," he continued walking. "I see it..." He paused as he heard the Kia's engine start. "Something's up."

Before he could move, the vehicle was backing out of its space and beginning the four-point-turn necessary to leave the lot.

"We can't let it get away!"

"I got it!" Sean heard the FBI car's engine start. "Just cover me." And then Gannon was moving, pulling her car in front of the Kia, forcing it to stop.

Sean saw movement in the suspect vehicle's front seat. He began to run, anxious to reach the two cars before...

The Kia suddenly backed away from the FBI car and gunned its engine, pulling onto the grass and speeding toward the road. Gannon tried to back up quickly enough to block it but it was no use—before she could get in front of the other car is was past, throwing up grass and loose soil as it skidded out into the street.

"Follow it!" Sean yelled, jumping into the passenger seat.

Gannon nodded and floored the gas pedal, expertly drifting across the grass and onto the road.

"I see him," she called out touching a button on the steering wheel. "Call headquarters!" She intoned, smiling. "I love that feature! Saves so much dialing!"

A *buzz* came from the speaker in her dashboard followed, a moment later, by a voice. "FBI— Malcolm speaking."

"Jeremy, this is Gannon—our suspect car is on the run. I have it in sight but I don't know the area around here too well..."

"Our backup is still nearly ten miles away." Sean heard the man on the line talking to someone else in the room. "Duncan says it's up to you— follow if you can but don't take any major risks."

"Yeah," Gannon skidded around a corner as the Kia made a sudden turn. "No major risks— whatever that means."

"Stay on the line—we'll vector the backup to your location."

"Roger that," she glanced at Sean. "What's your feeling on this?"

"Catch him if you can." His eyes were locked on the fleeing Kia. "We're not going to get any information from the one who tried to kill Ms. Nielson."

"I guess not." Gannon gave the car a bit more gas. "Okay, I'll do what I can..." She suddenly smiled. "You know, I always wanted to do this!"

"Do what?"

"Car chase through the city—followed by a big gun battle."

"I'd prefer to avoid the gun battle."

"Really," she raised an eyebrow, eyes still on the road ahead. "Your file says you're a hell of a shot!"

"You read my file?"

43

"Of course," she made another turn. "The freeway is only a couple of miles away."

"And if he gets there, the traffic will cut his speed in half!"

"Maybe not," Gannon glanced toward Sean. "What time is it?"

"I don't know..." He glanced at the console, found the clock. "Says it's about ten after eleven..."

"Not lunchtime yet," Gannon ran the tip of her tongue over her lip. "Rush hour is past..." She nodded. "Freeway might be clear."

"Might?"

"Well, if there was an accident or construction, it'll be backed up." She shrugged. "But otherwise, it'll be clear in both directions."

"That's great." Sean looked at the speeding Kia. "Any chance of reaching it before we get to the Freeway?"

"Afraid not."

The Kia suddenly turned right and disappeared from sight.

"That's the entrance!" Gannon braked and followed. "Let's hope..."

They came up the entry ramp—and found no traffic at all.

"Crap!" Sean leaned forward. "I can barely see him!"

"We can fix that." Gannon slammed the pedal down to the floor—and grinned. "High speed chase now!" She glanced at Sean. "Cool!"

"Yeah..." Sean pulled his cell phone and called his partner. "Frank?" He nodded. "The driver made it to the Freeway—we in pursuit—don't know how long until we get backup—you want to handle that?" He nodded at Farrell's response. "Good—I'll keep you posted on what happens."

He clicked the phone off.

"Okay Ms. Gannon," he looked at the young woman behind the wheel. "Let's see just how good a driver you are!" He pointed at the Kia. "Catch up to that thing—let me get a shot at the driver."

"Yes sir!" Her grin widened as the car leapt forward. "Anything you say, sir!"

Sean sat back in his seat as the speedometer hit ninety...

***

"What do you mean, you don't know where they are!" Frank Farrell snarled into his phone. "Don't they both have phones? Doesn't the car—one of your cars—have a radio?" I know they called for backup—where is that?"

Frank wasn't too worried about his partner—Sean could take care of himself—but paired with an unknown quantity—an FBI agent who had never worked the kind of cases Sean and Frank were accustomed to...

Anything can happen!

"Get me a car," his voice was lower now, deadly serious. "Right now."

He hung up before the Agent-in Charge at the Los Angeles office had time to reply.

***

"Where are we?" Sean asked as Gannon swept past a number of slower vehicles. "What happened to our backup?"

"I think we outran them." She nodded toward the GPS map on the car's console. "We're on I-5 and approaching San Clemente..."

"Isn't that close to the beach?"

"It's also close to San Diego—if our friend up ahead," she nodded at the car still in front of them. "Can reach the border..."

"All right," Sean pulled out his cell. "Let's see if we can get the cavalry on the job.

"Good luck," she answered. "If they really wanted to find us, they'd be here by now."

"You think your boss is dragging his heels?"

"He *does* think he should be the one in charge..."

"I'll have to have a talk with him," he punched in Farrell's number. "After we catch that guy!"

***

Frank was just about to call the Los Angeles office again when his phone buzzed, the Caller ID showing it to be Sean.

"Sean!" Farrell pushed the phone against his ear. "Where are you? What's going on?"

"Thought I'd ask you the same thing," the younger agent replied, his voice steady. "My backup hasn't arrived and Ms. Gannon suggests that her boss isn't in a mood to cooperate."

"Yeah, I got that impression too." Farrell took a deep breath. "Are you in real danger?"

"Well, Gannon's got us up over ninety miles an hour on a California Freeway..." Frank heard a chuckle. "But she's a pretty good driver and I think we're safe enough—I'm just worried about catching this guy before he gets somewhere we can't follow."

"I'm going to get a chopper—don't do anything foolish--but stop that guy—and try to keep him alive."

"Will do." Sean sounded pleased. "See you soon."

The connection went dead.

***

"All right," Sean smiled as Gannon maneuvered around a pair of trucks. "My partner is on the way."

"How long?"

"We can't wait for him." Sean looked at the speeding car still ahead of them. "I know you can drive—think you can knock that bastard off the road?"

"I've never done that..."

"Hey," he smiled. "I'll bet that' s not the first time you said that."

"True," she smiled back. "Where would you like to put him?"

"On the sand, I think." Sean looked to his right. "I'd like to take him alive and that might make it easier."

"Okay," she stomped hard on the gas pedal, pinning it to the floor. "Let's see if I can work this out..."

47

"You <u>did</u> take the FBI driving course, right?" Sean asked as the car flashed forward.

"Scheduled to take it next month," Gannon whipped past another truck. "They didn't have an opening before that..."

"I'll tell them you don't need it," Sean's feet braced as Gannon pulled one late to the right, skittering just a bit. "Why waste the time?"

"Hold on," she steered toward the Kia which was now just ahead and on the right. "I'll try a 'Pitt' maneuver..."

The car steadied, pulling up on the Kia's rear bumper. Sean saw the driver look into his side mirror...

"Do it now! He knows you're coming!"

Gannon nodded and once again goosed the gas pedal, this time steering her front bumper into the back left quarter of the Kia.

The two cars met with a thump...

"Again!" Sean yelled as he saw the Kia slew a little before regaining traction...

Gannon hit the back quarter again—harder this time. The FBI vehicle shuddered a bit—but the Kia reacted violently, skidding to the right as the driver frantically tried to correct.

He couldn't quite manage it—the right hand wheels hit the sand at the edge of the Freeway's pavement—and the Kia was instantly airborne, cartwheeling across the sand.

Gannon braked hard, fighting the wheel as the FBI vehicle shook...

Then it was under control and accelerating onto the sand, skidding as it turned toward the Kia which had come to rest on the driver side, smoke pouring out of the engine compartment...

"Cover me," Sean unbuckled his seat belt. "Remember, we want him alive!"

And then he was gone, rushing across the sand, pistol in hand, as he raced to get into a position from which he could see the Kia's driver.

Sean was within a hundred feet of the Kia when the passenger side door suddenly popped upward and a head and shoulders appeared—quickly followed by a pair of hands holding an AK-47.

"Crap!" Sean cut to one side and dove behind some low rocks just as the Kalashnikov opened up.

CHAPTER SIX

Frank Farrell was pissed as his helicopter sped over the freeway. It had taken two calls—the second to Mary Max—to get the local Agent-in-Charge to send the chopper to pick him up. That had cost valuable time—something that Frank suspected they did not have a great deal of.

They were near the Nixon Library in San Clemente when he saw the smoke.

"Over there," he pointed to his right. "There are two cars off the road...."

"I see them," the pilot pulled up on his cyclic, slowing the helicopter. "I'll get over them..."

"Look out!" Closer now, Farrell could see a man's head and shoulders atop one of the cars—this one overturned. The man had a rifle and was firing into the sand in the direction of another car. "That's our guy!"

"That Kalashnikov can take us down," he glanced at Farrell. "I really don't want to get within its range if I can avoid it."

"Don't worry," Frank smiled. "My partner's down there—he'll take care of that gun." His smile disappeared as he looked the situation over. *C'mon, Sean—don't make me a liar!* He thought.

***

Gannon watched, wide-eyed, as Sean approach the overturned Kia. She had been surprised when the top half of the driver suddenly appeared—and shocked when he produced a rifle and began firing.

Then her training took over and her sidearm was in her hand as she dropped out of the driver's door, keeping herself behind cover. She quickly crawled up behind the left front tire until she could see around it. She took careful aim, inhaled once, then squeezed the trigger...

***

I'm in deep shit! Sean told himself as he tried to dig into the sand far enough to avoid the bullets coming his way. *There's no real cover here and...*

He frowned as he heard a helicopter approaching.

Frank! He snatched a look. *He did manage to get a chopper!* He bit his lip. *Now what do I do?*

The Kalashnikov ran dry at that exact moment and Sean reacted without thought. He rose from his meager cover and sprinted hard toward the wrecked car.

He saw the driver drop the spent magazine, saw him insert a fresh one...

I'm done, he dropped to the ground, still twenty yards from the car and brought his own weapon up. *He's going to nail me before I can do anything!*

He saw the muzzle of the AK-47 raise, point in his direction...

Shots rang out from behind him, one *spanged* against the roof of the wrecked car just inches from the gunman's hands. The man pulled back involuntarily, opening himself as a target...

51

Sean didn't hesitate—he fired instantly, putting two rounds into the man's chest.

The AK-47 dropped from suddenly nerveless hands.

*I **did** want to take him alive.* Sean thought as he stood, pistol still fixed on the now-limp body hanging over the side of the car. *But it was him or me and,* he shook his head. *I'd rather it be him.*

"Are you all right?" Gannon yelled from behind him.

"Yeah," he turned toward the girl and waved. "I think you just saved my life." He smiled. "Nice shooting."

He turned back to the overturned car—just in time to see the driver suddenly move, producing a hand grenade.

And pulling the pin...

Sean hit the sand just as the grenade went off.

***

"You okay?" Sean slowly opened his eyes to see Frank Farrell kneeling next to him.

"Yeah," Sean grimaced as he spoke. "Got a hell of a headache though."

"We'll get some aspirins..."

"Gannon!" He sat up quickly—and immediately regretted it. He grabbed his aching head with both hands but still struggled to look back at the FBI car. "Is she okay?"

"She is," a familiar voice said from just behind him.

He turned to see Jennifer Gannon sitting on the sand just behind him, closing what looked like a regulation first-aid kit.

"I was sure you were a goner!" She shook her head. "You are some kind of crazy!"

"I had to take out that rifle before somebody got hurt." Sean moved his jaw from side to side, trying to make sure that it was still properly attached. "I should have been more careful—that grenade surprised me." He tried to turn toward the wrecked car. "Any way we're going to get any intel from the vehicle?"

"I doubt it," Farrell told him. "Unless the fire department gets here really fast."

"Fire?" Sean turned toward the wreck, saw the blaze. "I wouldn't have believed they had that much fuel left."

"I think it was prepped to burn," Farrell told him. "The driver was supposed to light it up when he switched cars." He grinned. "He didn't figure he'd be followed by you guys."

"It was all for nothing," Sean shook his head—grimaced again at the sudden pain. "We needed him alive."

"Sometimes you don't get what you want." Farrell put a hand on his partner's shoulder. "C'mon, let's get you back to town—you need to see a doctor."

"No," Sean started to shake his head—thought better of it—and put a hand into his pocket. "I have to look through this."

"I thought I told you..."

53

"I'm the computer guy—I make those decisions," he looked into Farrell's face. "Right *Partner*?"

The older man shrugged. "I guess you do at that." He stood up and reached a hand down for his partner. "C'mon, let's get you back."

"I'll drive back with Gannon," Sean grinned. "She got me this far."

"As you wish," Farrell shrugged. "I'll get the chopper back and meet you at the hotel."

Sean nodded and pulled himself upright, wobbling for a moment. "C'mon, Gannon." He smiled at his companion. "Let's see what the freeway looks like at normal speed."

"Crowded," she told him. "Crowded and slow."

"I seem to have lots of time," he smiled. "Thanks to you."

A moment later they were in the car and heading toward the city...

54

CHAPTER SEVEN

It was still early enough to allow them to drive back to LA in a reasonable amount of time. Gannon drove up to the doorway of the Omni and waited for Sean to get out.

He hesitated, hand on the door…

"Gannon—Jennifer," he smiled. "You've done a good job for us and I think you should at least be there to see if we found anything." He pursed his lips for a moment, thinking, then: "Park the car and come up with me—you deserve to know if anything is there."

Ten minutes later (the parking lot was pretty full), Gannon was making coffee on the hotel brewer while Sean began going through the information he'd taken from Crowdstrike.

Farrell wasn't back yet.

"This is interesting…" Sean stared at his screen. "These two 'Russian' agents that Crowdstrike has identified accessed the internet from inside the US." He made a note. "Have to look into that." He scrolled through more data. "Here are a bunch of those e-mails Secretary Clinton kept in her own server." He shook his head. "I'd like to know how she got away with that…"

He froze.

"Oh shit!" He leaned forward. "This is nearly five weeks old!" He looked at his watch. "What time does your boss leave the office?"

"Five on the dot," she had finished the coffee and was bringing a cup Sean's way. "Why?"

"I think I'm gonna need a secure line." He looked at the information in front of him. "Right away!"

Gannon put the coffee down on the desk. "I'll see if anyone's in the commo office," she pulled out her phone. "You're going to need permission from the Agent-in-Charge to send messages after hours."

"My boss will handle that," Sean pulled out his own phone. "I'll get Frank to call her." He dialed a number. "He knows her better than I do and we're damn sure going to disturb her dinner..."

***

Frank Farrell was still in the process of 'enjoying' Los Angeles traffic patterns. The helicopter had returned to Van Nuys airport—near Los Angeles International. It had taken some time to work its way through the traffic pattern and land, leaving Farrell on the ground just as rush hour started in earnest.

He considered a van—but finally opted to take an Uber—there were a lot of them in the LA area and he thought it might be his best chance of getting back to the hotel in a reasonable amount of time.

He was wrong, traffic was bumper to bumper as far as the eye could see—each car holding only one person. Farrell settled back in his seat, prepared to nap as the Uber inched its way through traffic. He'd finally managed to get somewhat comfortable when his phone rang.

"Sean?" Farrell frowned at the voice coming from the device. "I'm caught in traffic—big time—and I can't really talk..."

He listened for a long moment.

"All right, have Gannon take you to headquarters—I'll contact Mary Max and get the ball rolling." He nodded. "Meet you there."

He hung up and leaned over the seat. "I need to change my destination—can you do that?"

"Sure," the driver, a blonde girl wearing too much makeup smiled. "Where do you want me to take you?"

"I need to go to FBI headquarters-- 11000 Wilshire Boulevard."

"Not that far from the Omni," the girl nodded. "Okay, I'll take you there." She glanced at him. "It might take a while..."

"I understand," he settled back into his seat. "But I don't understand how you people can live like this!"

"Hey," she chuckled. "Traffic is pretty light today—you should see it on a Friday!"

Farrell shook his head and glared at his phone as he called up Mary Max's cell number. There was no chance that he'd get a nap now...

***

An hour later, Farrell and Sean were in the FBI communications room talking to Mary Max on a conference call.

"So what did you find that's so important?" Mary Max asked. "I really don't like stepping on a local Agent-In-Charge."

"He's a *dick*, Mary Max," Farrell muttered. "You know that as well as I do."

57

"*Dick* or not, he *is* in charge." Mary Max paused. "But I'll make sure that if you need to reach me again," another pause. "Or if you need faster transport and backup, there will be no hesitation on his part." Farrell smiled at Sean. "Now, what did you find?"

"I was able to secure the data that the DNC passed to Crowdstrike." Sean hesitated. "<u>All</u> of the data—if you understand what I mean."

The sound of a sigh came through the speaker. "I suppose it would be a bad idea to ask how you got it?"

"Yes Ma'am."

"All right," she sighed again. "Tell me what you found."

"I found an e-mail from a State Department employee in Yemen referring to the disappearance of the ABQAIQ—a Saudi Oil and Chemical tanker. The employee was worried about the reaction of the owners and sent the message as a heads-up." Sean paused for a deep breath. "It got bounced from communications to the Secretary's associate—and stopped there."

"Stopped?"

"Yes, Ma'am, stopped. The only reason I found it was because the e-mails that were found in Mr. Wiener's computer were part of the package that went to Crowdstrike."

"Okay," Mary Max's voice held more interest now. "And what's so important about this—what was the name? ABQUICK?"

"ABQAIQ, ma'am. When I was in Dr. Ramnarain's office, I saw references to a number of plans—one of them had the heading ABQAIQ."

"I see..." Mary Max took a deep breath. "Did you see what the plan for this ship was?"

"No Ma'am, I never really got to examine any of his files in detail—and you'll remember that he destroyed everything when he moved hideouts..."

"I seem to recall something like that."

Whatever the plan was, the name <u>was</u> there—and seeing it again made me worry..."

"I can understand that." Mary Max hesitated. "I'll see if any of our agencies knows where this..."

"The ABQAIQ, Ma'am."

"Where the ship in question might be at this time. I'll contact you as soon as I have an answer." She hesitated. "I'll text you the information—I don't see any reason to bother our friends in the LA FBI any further, do you?"

"Well, Ma'am." Sean started.

"No, Mary Max," Farrell leaned past him, holding up a hand to silence him. "We won't bother the FBI about anything at all—unless you tell us to do so."

"Good enough." Mary Max sighed again. "I'll get back to you as soon as I can." She hesitated. "And Sean..."

"Ma'am?"

"Please look for the information I tasked you to find—the proof of any Russian collusion in our recent election."

"I'll look again, ma'am, but I didn't see anything concrete in my initial pass."

"Look carefully."

"Yes Ma'am, I will."

"Good." Another hesitation. "What time is it there?"

"Just after six, Ma'am." Farrell answered.

"Get some dinner—I should have something for you by morning."

"Ma'am?"

"Sean."

"Can I invite Ms. Gannon—our driver/liaison with the local FBI join us? She saved my life in the shootout this afternoon."

"There was a shootout?"

"You'll have our report first thing in the morning, Ma'am." Farrell quickly filled in. "It happened just an hour or two ago."

"Shootout." They heard a deep breath. "And you didn't feel the need to lead with that." Another deep breath. "You two lead interesting lives—and I'll look forward to that report—I'm sure it'll be fascinating reading."

"Yes Ma'am."

"Go have that dinner—and by all means take your FBI friend with you—I'll okay the expense."

"Thank you, Ma'am." Sean smiled. "She's young and new to all this but she's done a great job so far."

"Put her full name in the report," Mary Max told them. "Maybe I can find a way to reward her."

"That would be nice," Sean nodded. "She's really shows promise."

"Stick with the girlfriend you have, Sean." Mary Max's voice was dry. "You're not the sort to handle more than one at a time."

"Never crossed my mind, Ma'am."

"Good, then you'll have dinner and I'll see about this missing freighter—we'll speak tomorrow morning."

60

"Yes Ma'am." Sean smiled.

"Have a good night, Ma'am."

"Good night!" Mary Max snorted. "I'm going to spend much of it trying to get this ship tracked down!"

The line went dead.

"That went well," Sean stated.

"Yeah," Farrell glared at him. "But now I have to write a report!"

"You'd have done that anyway." Sean shrugged. "I'll help you—after we have dinner."

"Where shall we go?"

"Let's ask Gannon, she's a local..."

The two men strolled out of the FBI secure room...

***

Your memory is good, Sean. Mary Max's text had arrived early the next morning. *Transport will be waiting at Long Beach Airport at 1400. See you soon.*

"What do you think that means?" Farrell asked. "Did she find anything?"

"She must have found <u>something</u>," Sean yawned. He had spent a big chunk of the night going through the data he'd gotten from Crowdstrike. "How about you? Anything on the guys with the guns?"

"FBI still hasn't made an identification. Neither man had a wallet or any form of ID on them." Farrell shrugged. "Guns were pretty common..."

"How about the clothing?" Sean asked. "They were pretty snappy dressers."

"Suits were made in central Europe—anywhere from Bulgaria to Belgium," he shook his head. "No help there."

"The suppressor?"

"That was odd," Farrell pulled the device out of his pocket. "This is homemade—by someone who knew what he was doing. The FBI couldn't connect it with anyone in particular—they're hoping the boys in Washington will have better luck."

"Good enough," Sean yawned again.

"How much sleep *did* you get?"

"Maybe an hour," Sean shrugged. "No big deal—I'll sleep on the plane—which reminds me," he picked up his phone. "We'll need transport to Long Beach."

"You calling Ms. Gannon again?"

"Yeah," he looked at Farrell. "Why?"

"No reason," the older man grinned. "It's just that I thought you <u>had</u> a girlfriend."

"I told you I wasn't sure." He sent a text to Gannon's number. "Besides, Jen was tasked with driving us wherever we want to go."

"So," Farrell smiled. "It's 'Jen' now, is it?"

"Let it go, Frank." Sean shook his head. "Just let it go."

"Okay," Farrell held up his hands in surrender. "Did you find anything in the computer data?"

"Nothing that indicates the Russians did what everyone is saying they did. Hell, if Crowdstrike is wrong about the identity of these two hackers, there's no connection with Russia at all!"

"Well, at least we can tell Mary Max that much!"

"Not that it'll do any good with the circus in Congress."

"Not our problem." Farrell took a step back. "C'mon, let's get packed."

"Already done." Sean looked at him. "I told you I didn't get much sleep."

"It took you all night to go through the data?"

"No," Sean shook his head. "It took me all night to find the ABQAIQ—or at least to find where it was two weeks ago."

"Tell me about it while we're on the way," Farrell stood up. "I've got to pack and get some breakfast."

"Breakfast," Sean smiled. "Sounds like an idea." He waved at his partner. "I'll see you in the restaurant."

"Don't eat everything!" Farrell yelled at Sean's back. "Leave some for me!"

***

The Lockheed Jetstar 731 waiting for them at the airport had Air Force markings but was, quite clearly, an antique.

"I thought they retired these twenty years ago," Farrell muttered as he climbed the ladder and entered the aircraft.

"Maybe it's all that was available," Sean followed him, pausing to wave goodbye to Gannon. "Any reason to think it won't get us home?"

63

"This'll do the job all right," Farrell grinned at the uniformed stewardess waiting inside. "It'll just burn a lot more fuel doing so."

"We're not paying for it," Sean found a comfortable seat that reclined enough to let him lay almost flat—then yawned hugely. "Wake me when we get there."

"I'll wake you when we make our first stop for gas," Farrell grinned. "Or maybe I'll wait for the second stop—or the third..."

Sean shook his head, put an arm across his eyes, and was asleep before the little jet began its takeoff run...

***

As the Jetstar sped across the US, another vessel—a tanker—wallowed in heavy weather in the Atlantic.

"Allah is angry with us!" Abdalmalek Farouq groaned, the constant rolling of the ship keeping his stomach in a constant state of upset.

"On the contrary," Mansur Al-Enezi smiled. "He shields us from the Infidel's accursed eyes in the sky." He patted Abdalmalek on the shoulder. "His hand is over us!"

"I had not thought of it that way," Farouq nodded. "You are right! I..." A sudden roll of the deck pitched the wiry man against the wall. "I wish he had his hand over my stomach!"

"Be of good cheer, my friend." Mansur smiled. "In two days we will be within sight of our target."

"And after that..." Abdalmalek held onto a railing as the ship moved again.

"After that we will be with Allah in Paradise!"

"Ins-Allah!" Abdalmalek repeated, holding up a hand to reinforce his statement.

The upheld hand unbalanced him enough that he was tossed off his feet when the next wave hit...

***

"The Coast Guard says that the ABQAIQ does not exist," Mary Max said, greeting them. "They say it sunk more than two years ago."

"The Coast Guard is wrong," Sean opened his laptop and plugged into the audio-visual plug in front of his spot at the conference table. "The ABQAIQ was acquired from a Saudi crew in Yemeni waters two and a half years ago," he found the file and uploaded a picture of the ship in question. "The Saudi's put in an insurance claim with Lloyds—which is why our Coast Guard believes it was destroyed."

"Go on."

"It took a little time but I finally found this." He hit another key and a new image appeared..

"Is that the same ship? Farrell leaned forward. "It looks different..."

"The CIA came across this about a year ago." Sean put the two images side by side. "This was in a dock somewhere in Indonesia." Sean rotated the two images. "It certainly looks like the same ship— the CIA thought so and passed the information to Lloyds and the former owners in Saudi Arabia but, as the insurance had been paid..." Sean shrugged.

"Is that ship still in a dock?"

"Nope," Sean shook his head. "This vessel has been re-named '*BATAVIAN BELLE*'—a name no Indonesian would think of picking but one that seems innocuous enough."

"If this really is the ABQAIQ," Mary Max leaned forward. "Why do you believe it's so dangerous?"

"I've pieced this much together from some of the notes I found. Three or four years ago, while he was still working for the US Government, Dr. Ramnarain conceived of a plan to use a tanker as a giant fuel-air bomb." He looked at Mary Max. "It'd be easy enough to do. He presented the plan to the CIA but they said they had no need of such a bomb." Sean spread his arms. "It's possible that he then took his plan to someone else—there're indications he had contact with Al Qaeda..."

"That would be dangerous," Farrell nodded. "All you have to do is partially fill a tanker with fuel and let that fuel sit for a while until the vapors it gives off fills the tank." He looked at Sean. "It wouldn't take much to ignite it and..." His eyes widened as he thought it through. "If they get the proportions right, the explosion would be devastating!"

"I checked various CIA reports and the most recent set of satellite images. The 'BATAVIAN BELLE' is no longer anywhere in Indonesian waters. I assumed it went to sea and tried to find it." He shook his head. "The weather over the Pacific right now is very bad—lots of cloud cover and rain..." He shrugged. "I found several possible targets using Infrared but I can't be sure which one is ours."

"How serious is this?"

"A ship loaded the way Sean suggests..." Farrell shrugged. "it could easily take out the locks of the Panama Canal—make it useless for," he shrugged. "A year? Two?"

"It could do a lot worse if it got into a port—think of a bomb like that going off in Houston or Los Angeles," he shook his head. "Or New York..."

"All right," Mary Max nodded. "We clearly have to find this ship—and quickly." She looked at Sean. "Where did you come across the original data on this?"

Two years ago, someone in Saudi Arabia passed the information about the tanker to the State Department. It was moved up the ladder until it got to the Secretary's Aide," Sean shrugged. "Near as I can tell, it went no further. I found it in the data from her husband's laptop—the stuff the FBI was looking into in October."

"But they didn't find this."

"Not their fault, Ma'am—if I hadn't seen the file name on Dr. Ramnarain's desk, I wouldn't have found it either."

"I'm glad you did." Mary Max stood. "I'll get some people working on this right now—you two get some rest and prepare your report." Her mouth curled into a smile. "I'm looking forward to hearing about this gunfight..."

CHAPTER EIGHT

Mansur Al-Enezi smiled as he entered the bridge of the ABQAIQ. "It is a beautiful day, my friend!" He looked through the glass that surrounded the ship's controls. "One could not ask for a better day!"

"I disagree," Abdalmalek answered. "I would have liked at least another day of bad weather. It is too clear." He looked upwards. "The Infidel's 'satellites' might be able to see us."

"What does it matter?" Mansur shrugged. "They have no idea what we have planned—they know nothing about this ship!"

"Do not underestimate the Infidels," the taller Arab answered. "They have eyes everywhere and are not easy to fool."

"We are in Allah's hands, my friend." Mansur smiled. "And he has smiled on us so far!"

"Yes he has." Abdalmalek sighed. "And I pray that he continues to do so."

***

He did not—and so, two hours later, in the small conference room assigned to Mary Max...

"One of our satellites picked this up very early this morning," Mary Max sent the image to the large monitor screen that filled the wall behind her. "It's unidentified—running no flag and not communicating in any way." She turned to Farrell and Sean who were watching intently. "The Navy is going to send a Destroyer to take a look." She smiled. "Would you two like to join them?"

***

"The USS Higgins," Sean read off his laptop. "DDG-76) is an Arleigh Burke-class destroyer named for Colonel William R. Higgins."

"I remember hearing about him," Farrell said. "Bush gave Colonel Higgins the Presidential Citizen's Award and then named a ship," he looked down. "That ship, after the Colonel."

That ship was some five hundred feet beneath the helicopter which had ferried Sean and Farrell from San Diego.

Now it had to set down on the postage stamp which was the Higgins landing pad.

"I've never done this before," Sean called out over through the communications system built into his helmet. "What's it like landing on one of those things."

"In a calm sea," one of the pilots told him. "It's a piece of cake."

"Is this a calm sea?" Sean, peering out, could see some wave action and the ship was certainly pitching back and forth.

"Not dead calm," the pilot smiled back at him. "But not too bad." He shrugged. "We'll have you down in a few minutes..." The smile widened. "One way or another—you can swim, right?"

"Don't let them scare you, Sean." Farrell shook his head. "They do this pretty much every day of the week."

"Your friend's right," the pilot responded. "We do this all the time," his smile grew crooked. "And we almost always make it with no trouble."

"Thanks," Sean smiled back. "Thanks a lot."

"Come on, Sean." Farrell looked at his partner. "You jump out of airplanes!"

"Yeah," Sean bit his lower lip. "But there are no sharks under you when you jump out of an airplane."

"All right, Gentlemen," the pilot announced. "We have clearance to land. Make sure you're buckled in."

Sean pulled his five-point harness a little tighter and watched as the helicopter descended rapidly, drifting to the right until it was directly over the Destroyer's landing pad. A moment later there was a more-or-less gentle *bump*—and they were down.

"We have to head right back," the pilot told them. "Would you drop the mail off for us?" He held up a cloth bag.

"Sure," Farrell took it from him. "Happy to do it."

"We'll see you guys another time," the pilot made a motion and the door alongside Sean slid open. "Good hunting."

A moment later Sean and Farrell were on the pad watching the helicopter lift smoothly away.

"Don't think I'd want their job," Sean said in an undertone.

"I doubt they'd want ours," Farrell turned toward the young officer who'd come out to meet them. "Lieutenant..."

"Tinder, sir. Lieutenant JG Raymond Tinder." The young man stiffened, almost saluting. "The

70

Captain's compliments and will you join him in the wardroom."

"Of course," Farrell held out the mail pouch. "And would you see that this gets delivered to the men?"

"My pleasure, sir," the young man took the bag and smiled. "This way."

The wardroom, it turned out, was forward of the landing pad. Sean and Farrell followed their guide as he led them down a staircase then down a long corridor.

"The wardroom is below and behind the bridge," he told them as they walked. "It's where the officers have their meals and take breaks while on duty."

"I see," Sean nodded. "And Combat Control?"

"It's amidships where it has the most protection." The young man smiled. "It's my station if we go to General Quarters."

"You're a sonar specialist, right?"

"How did you know that?"

Sean tapped his laptop, now packed into s carry bag he'd hung over his shoulder. "I went through the ship's company on the trip out here." He raised an eyebrow. "I was hoping you could show me the system while we're aboard."

"Of course," Tinder smiled. "Assuming the Captain approves."

"I'll be sure to ask," Sean smiled back. "And hope we have the time."

"Can I ask what your visit is all about?"

"I'm sorry," Farrell interjected. "We can't tell you that unless the Captain approves—I will tell you that it's a classified operation and could be vitally important."

"Understood, sir." The lieutenant turned a last corner and pulled a door on his right open. "The Wardroom, Gentlemen."

***

The Wardroom was comfortable enough. A table, big enough for eight, sat in the middle. There was a refrigerator on one wall, a bridge repeater on another, and a large TV screen on the third.

Three officers sat around the table sipping coffee.

"Gentlemen," the one at the head of the table stood. "I'm Lt. Commander Quickel, commanding the Higgins."

Farrell stepped forward to take the man's hand. "Glad to meet you, sir. I'm Frank Farrell and this," he nodded to his side. "Is Sean Piper, my partner."

"Aren't you a little young?"

"Maybe," Sean smiled. "But my Boss is happy with the job I do—and that's what really counts, right?"

"Indeed, Mr. Piper." Quickel smiled. "Welcome aboard." He waved a hand for them to take seats. "Now, just what is this all about? I have orders to track down a small tanker," he looked at the two agents. "And to follow your instructions when we find it."

"The tanker," Farrell nodded to Sean who opened his laptop, found the wireless access, and put an image of the ship in question on the big TV

72

screen. "Is called the BATAVIAN BELLE now—but I believe it was once the ABQAIQ."

"Renaming ships is bad luck," an officer on the right side of the table muttered.

"So I've heard," Sean smiled. "Although it didn't seem to stop the British and French from doing it continually during their various wars."

"Hmmph," the officer looked at Sean, brow furrowed, then: "You're right, Mr. Piper." A smile appeared. "And I should remember my own history lessons."

"ABQAIQ or BATAVIAN BELLE," the Captain interjected. "What's so important about that ship?"

"If we're right, "Farrell told him. "It's been turned into a huge fuel/air bomb and is enroute to attack the Canal."

"I see." The Captain nodded as he reached for a phone. "Bridge," he said. "Captain." He looked around the table. "Increase speed to two thirds and double the radar watch. Let me know if anything turns up."

Sean saw the bridge repeater on one wall change, the half-speed replaced by two-thirds. The ship shuddered as more power was fed to the propellers.

"Now, gentlemen." The Captain stood up. "I think I'll go up to the Bridge and see what I can see." He looked at Sean and Farrell. "I'll have Lt. Tinder show you to your quarters and put him at your service to take you anywhere you want to go." He smiled. "You have the run of the ship."

"Thank you sir," Farrell stood as well. "I think we'll take a few minutes to familiarize ourselves with the Higgins."

"Good," the Captain headed for the door. "Officer's mess is at four bells—six PM, although you can get a meal or a snack anytime you please." He nodded to the phone. "Just call for the Steward—he'll take care of you."

"Thanks again, Captain." Farrell smiled. "And good hunting!"

***

It was Mansur Al-Enezi's turn to smile as he stepped onto the bridge. "Allah smiles on us, brother!" He told his companion. "This storm will allow us to get very close to our target without being seen."

"If you say so," Abdalmalek shook his head. "I would still prefer the sun overhead rather than this constant darkness."

"One more day, brother." Mansur tapped on the compass housing.

"Why do you do that?"

The Arab smiled and shook his head. "I do not know," he spread his hands. "But I have seen it done many times in the infidel's movies." He shrugged. "It must be good for something!"

"You watch too many of those movies!" Abdalmalek shook his head. "Better you study the holy books!"

"I have read the Qur'an," the other man answered, eyes serious. "I know the words of the prophet."

"That is good," Mansur nodded. "And soon we will have obeyed his greatest command—we shall strike at the very heart of the Infidel's strength in this hemisphere!"

"Ins'Allah," the other man smiled. "Allah willing!"

The *Abqaiq* nee *Batavian Belle* continued steadily on course, the storm hanging overhead as it went.

***

"We think that this is your tanker." An image, colored in tones of green and red appeared on the main screen of the Combat Command Center.

"I thought there was a storm over that part of the Pacific?" Farrell said.

"This is infrared imaging," the Captain smiled. "You didn't think a little storm would blind us, did you?"

"It looks like the right hull shape," Sean had moved closer to the screen, studying the imaging. "And it's in the right place." He turned to the Captain. "What do we do now?"

"We'll close in on her. When we're sure she's the Abqaiq, we'll fire a shot across her bow and board her."

"Won't that put your men in serious jeopardy?" Farrell frowned. "If they set off their 'bomb'..."

"It's our job, sir." The first officer put in. "What would you have us do?"

"I might have an idea," Sean bit his lower lip. "I know you have a helicopter aboard—do you have a parachute?"

"What would you want a parachute for?"

"Well," Sean smiled and leaned forward. "Once we know for sure that this is the target, I could..."

The officers crowded around the young agent, listening intently...

CHAPTER NINE

Four hours later, Sean was airborne, looking down at cloud cover so heavy that he couldn't make out the sea below.

"Can we see through this?" He asked the pilot.

"We have all kinds of sensors," the tactical sensor operator (TSO) told him. "We have a FLIR turret with laser designator," he pointed forward, and the full Aircraft Survival Equipment package which includes an ALQ-144 Infrared Jammer, an AVR-2 Laser Detector, and a pair of APR-39(V)2 Radar Detectors. If it's down there, we'll find it."

He peered at his IR screen. "In fact, I believe that's our target just coming into view."

"Let's make sure," Sean smiled. "Before we go to phase two of the plan." He tapped the co-pilot on the arm. "Can we overfly them to get a good look?"

"No problem," the rather short officer nodded at Sean. "We'll stay above the clouds—high enough so that he can't hear us." He nodded to the pilot who pulled back on his controls.

The helicopter began to rise.

"We should be overhead in ninety seconds," the TSO told Sean. "We can compare his configuration with the satellite image."

"Good," Sean looked at the screen. "How far behind is the Higgins?"

"Only about three nautical miles," the man grinned. "In this weather, there's no way the target can see her."

77

"Flying over target now!" The Co-Pilot announced.

Sean watched as the helicopter's infra-red sensors painted an image of the tanker on the screen. He compared the length and width of the vessel with the photo he had in his hand...

"Looks like our boys to me," he offered, handing the photo to the TSO.

"I concur." He said. "I'll send the info back to the Higgins." He looked at Sean. "Are you sure you want to do this?"

"We need to get information about this ship and who was behind it—if we blow her out of the water, we'll get nothing." He shrugged. "Besides, I can't let the Higgins get too close—if they blow her then..."

"I didn't think CIA gave a shit about us."

"I give a shit." He tapped the co-pilot on the shoulder. "Take us up!"

***

"Allah is still watching over us" Abdalmalek noted, watching the rain fall on the deck in front of the wheelhouse. "No one can see us in this weather!"

"How far to our target?" Mansur asked. "We must make arrangements to put the crew ashore before..."

"The crew will not go ashore," Abdalmalek's voice was hard. "They will go with us right into the target."

"But we told them..."

"They are good Muslims—they will be rewarded for what they are about to accomplish."

"I'm not sure that they will see it that way."

The taller man shrugged. "If you think they will be rebellious, get a weapon from the arms locker—and bring one for me."

"As you say."

"We will soon be in sight..." He grinned, gesturing at the rain. "Or, at least, within radio range of our target." His grin widened. "We will use the infidels own beacons to guide us to the target." He nodded. "Allah will be pleased!"

***

"All right," the TSO was looking into Sean's eyes. "Your altimeter is set to the current barometric readings—be careful, the clouds go down almost to the surface—you only have about ten or fifteen feet of ceiling."

"I'll have to open the 'chute while I'm still in the clouds." Sean nodded. "You're going to have to give me directional fixes."

"We'll do that—and give you some help with the altitude." The TSO looked at him again. "Are you sure you want to do this?"

"Somebody has to," Sean shrugged. "And I'm the only one who can."

"All right—get yourself set up by the door." He turned to the pilot. "Start the run."

The chopper turned toward the target.

"On course." The pilot intoned. "Two miles..."

Sean gave his gear one last check. He'd borrowed an M-4 from the Higgin's security detail and had it slung—safety on—across his chest.

Now he clicked the safety 'off'.

"One mile..."

Sean patted his sidearm, making sure it was still in place, then turned toward the door, sliding it open.

"five hundred yards..." The pilot was concentrating on his instruments now. "Four hundred. Three hundred..."

Sean leaned forward.

"Two hundred... One hundred..."

Before the man could speak, Sean had pushed himself out, going into a tuck to avoid any possible trouble with the rotors.

***

"He's out," The TSO reported. "Dropping right along the calculated glide path...":

Frank Farrell listened to the report before turning to the Captain of the Higgins. "Let's speed it up," he smiled. "We don't want to miss the party, now do we?""

Moments later the destroyer was making nearly thirty knots as it sped toward the targeted tanker...

***

"Crap!" Sean realized that it was going to be difficult to see anything. He'd been immediately soaked by the moisture in the clouds—that soaking

80

included his faceplate which meant that his vision was blurry at best.

I'm all right, he told himself. *Just follow the profile...*

His body was in a pike position, aimed toward what he hoped was the position of the tanker. He would stay in this position, moving fast and straight, until he was under two thousand feet. At that time, he would deploy his chute and hope for the best.

"Helo One to jumper," the voice was soft but distinct in Sean's earbud.

"Jumper here," he murmured. "Any problems?"

"You are on target and online." The voice was soft and clear. "Eight thousand feet and descending." There was a brief pause. "Higgins is on the way at flank speed."

"Roger that," Sean sighed as a thicker band of moisture coated his faceplate. "Lots of water in the air—I really can't see a thing."

"Roger that," the voice hesitated. "Don't worry—we'll guide you in."

"You'd better," Sean smiled. "Because I can't even see my altimeter."

"Roger—you are online and moving as predicted. Six thousand feet and descending..."

***

Muhammad Hasan stood on the afterdeck of the Abqaiq, trying to keep the cigarette in his hand shielded from the rain. He kept checking over his shoulder—smoking was considered *Haram*— forbidden—by many practitioners of Islam—

81

including the two men who were commanding this particular expedition.

I do not understand why the prophet disliked tobacco, Muhammad asked himself as he took a long drag. *It soothes the nerves and makes life on this accursed ship possible.*

He took another lungful of smoke, watching the rear door to the bridge intently—so intently that he didn't see the paravane explode through the clouds just behind him.

***

Too close! Sean yanked hard on his shrouds, trying desperately to slow himself down.

He'd broken through the clouds less than fifty feet from the tanker's fantail—and only about twenty feet above it.

Now he worried if he was too fast to land on the deck.

Those guys in the helicopter did a great job getting me this far, he told himself. *My turn now!*

He worked the lines hard, catching all the air he could and gulling his paravane out just enough to slow himself to a brisk walking pace. He was happy that the Higgins had the paravane aboard—if he'd had nothing but an old-style parachute, he'd be sure to go into the water—at least this way he had a fighting chance.

He was less than ten feet from the ship now—and only two or three feet above deck level—close enough to see a man standing there with his back pointed in his direction.

Tough to use the M-4 with one hand, he realized. *I'll have to chance the noise of a pistol shot.*

He drew his Glock from its holster, just over the deck, flicked the safety 'OFF'...

***

Mansur Al-Enezi was sitting in the Captain's chair, studying the waters ahead of him.

I can't see much, he noted. *But my radar track and GPS both say that I'm less than fifty miles from the entrance to the Infidel's canal.*

He smiled, thinking about what would happen to that canal after their little surprise.

Only fifty miles. He worried at his lower lip. Perhaps *I should awaken Abdalmalek—he'll surely want to be on the bridge when we enter the canal.* He stood up and turned toward the cabin door— then stopped himself.

It will take some time to cover fifty miles at the rate we're going. He smiled. *Might as well let him get some sleep...*

He settled back into the captain's chair—which creaked as he put his weight into it, loud enough that he did not hear the flat crack of Sean's pistol somewhere behind him.

***

Sean keyed on his radio as soon as he landed on the deck of the Abqaiq. "Jumper to Helo One..." He pushed the Arab overboard—followed by the paravane. "Anyone hear me?"

83

"Helo one here, you're loud and clear."

"I'm on board the tanker—tell the Captain that I'll report after I clear the bridge."

"Roger Jumper," the TSO quickly answered, then: "Any problems?"

"There was a crewman performing a forbidden act on the stern." Sean grinned and shrugged. "Allah did not warn him I was there."

"Roger that," the TSO chuckled. "Be careful with the bridge."

"I will--just make sure my back-up gets here on time." He adjusted the sling on the M-4, jacked a round into the chamber and trotted toward the ladder that, he knew, led to the bridge.

***

Mansur was watching the radar screen. There was something—a ship perhaps—moving toward them from behind. He wasn't quite sure what he should do—there was no way it could be an infidel warship and yet...

I'd better wake Abdalmalek, he decided. *He is more knowledgeable about such things than I am.* He had just risen to his feet when he heard a metal upon metal sound behind him.

He recognized it as the noise the outside hatch made when opened.

"I am glad you're awake, my friend," he turned, smiling, toward the hatch and, he assumed, Abdalmalek. He pointed toward the instruments. "There is something on the radar..."

He stopped, eyes widening, as he saw the rifle pointed at his chest.

84

"Stand right where you are!" Sean called out in his now-excellent Arabic. "Do not move!"

The Arab stared at him, shocked. "Who are you? Where do you come from?"

"On your knees," he gestured with the M-4. "Right there."

Masur stared at him, trying to decide what he could do. The emergency detonator was just behind him—alongside the radar set. If he could reach it...

"Down!" Sean's eyes were hard. "Right now!"

The man continued to stare at him—then his eyes widened and: "Abdalmalek! Beware!"

Sean cursed—but he had no options. He squeezed the trigger and put two rounds into the Arab then whirled toward the new threat—a second man entering the bridge from the interior of the ship. That man, taller and lighter-skinned than the other, took one look at him and turned to flee down the interior corridor.

Sean gave chase, speaking into his mike as he did so. "Hurry up! I left one Arab on the bridge but the other saw me do so and is running deeper into the ship. If he reaches the tanks..."

"We're only a few miles behind you, Sean." Farrell's calm voice answered. "We'll have boarders on that ship in ten minutes or less..."

"Hold the boarders until I can secure the tanker—if they blow it when you're too close, you'll lose too many men."

"Sean, you can't..."

"I can and I will," he reached the end of the corridor and went down a ladder. He could hear the sounds of the man preceding him echoing off the metal bulkheads. "Just hurry—I'll report when the ship is safe."

He sped up, eyes searching the dimness around him for the surviving Arab...

CHAPTER TEN

Abdalmalek ran as fast as his legs would carry him. He had seen the figure on the bridge shoot Mansur down before turning toward him. *A highly trained fighter,* he told himself. *One who knew better than to turn and leave an enemy behind him.*

Abdalmalek knew that he must be a member of one of America's elite units—and also knew that where there was one such, more would be nearby.

I have to get to the detonator! The tall Arab reached the opening and, skidding on the floor, made the turn. At first, he'd thought of using the switch on the bridge—but he had no chance to get by the armed Infidel. *I have to get to the hold,* he was breathing hard now—partially from the exertion, partially from fear. *I have to reach the controls before he catches me.*

The ladder he needed was just ahead. All he had to do was descend and access the circuit they had rigged to spark in the large tank...

He slipped on the fourth step down and fell the rest of the way. Pain flooded his lower back...

***

He's too far ahead of me! Sean realized. *If he beats me to whatever detonator they've set up...*

He heard a clatter to his right, followed by a curse in Arabic.

He went this way! Sean turned down the side corridor. *I can still catch him!* He saw the ladder just ahead. *I've got to hurry!*

He reached the ladder and turned to go down—but stopped in his tracks as the glare of a handgun appeared below and a bullet hit the ceiling right over his head.

Shit! Sean ducked and brought his M-4 around. It was too dark below to see anything but he couldn't just stand there. He switched the weapon to 'AUTO' and aimed it down the ladder before pulling the trigger.

He held it until the magazine was empty.

***

Abdalmalek held back a scream as he rolled over onto his stomach. He couldn't stand up—his back was burning with pain too intense for him to ignore. He saw the shadow of his pursuer at the top of the ladder and fired once...

He ducked as the rifle came up and began to fire—but there was nowhere to go. He shrieked as the first round hit him in the shoulder, then he was hit in the chest once, twice, three times...

He couldn't breathe. He tried to lift his pistol but it weighed too much.... He heard it clatter as it fell to the ground. He tried to find it but it was so dark...so very dark...

***

I think I got him, Sean thought as he reloaded his rifle. *But I don't have time to be careful while I*

88

find out. He stood up and swung his rifle back down toward the bottom of the ladder.

Nothing happened.

I've got to find the detonator before someone sets it off!

Sean let his rifle slip down on its sling while he slid down the ladder, grimacing as his feet came down in what was left of the Arab he'd been chasing.

I guess I got him, Sean wiped his right sole off on a scrap of cloth. *Now to find the fuel tank and the detonator...*

He hurried up the corridor...

***

"He must be deep inside the ship," the seaman at the radio told Farrell. "I can't get a signal."

"Crap," Farrell looked out at the rapidly enlarging silhouette of the tanker. "Keep trying."

He didn't wait to see the man acknowledge.

"We've got to board as soon as we can," Farrell joined the captain at the front of the bridge. "There's no telling how many men are aboard that..."

"I thought the idea was to let your partner make the bomb safe before we came too close." The Captain raised an eyebrow. "Has he radioed the all-clear?"

"We're not getting any reception," Farrell nodded toward the bigger ship. "He must be deep inside..."

"Where, I assume, he's defusing the bomb." The Captain shook his head. "I'm sorry, Mr.

Farrell, but I'm not going to get any closer until I get that all clear."

"I can order you to do it—you have been placed under my command you know."

"I know that," the young officer looked into Farrell's eyes. "But I'm hoping you won't do that. I'm hoping you have faith in your partner..."

"I do have faith," Farrell smiled crookedly. "But I still worry about him."

***

Half a mile away, Sean opened a hatch that, if he had read the ship's plans correctly, should lead into the main storage tank...

A quick smell told him he was in the right place.

This thing is saturated with gasoline vapors, he realized. *I don't think shooting would be a good idea...*

He slung the rifle across his back—making sure it was on 'SAFE', and stepped inside.

If I were a terrorist, where would I put an igniter? Sean asked himself. It had to be somewhere above the level of the fuel—and it had to be wired to a control on the bridge...

Sean looked around, trying to find anything that looked out of place.

There! He saw the metallic thing on top of one of the guard rails. *That must be it!*

He hurried forward.

"Hey!" A voice speaking Arabic came from behind him. "Who are you!"

Sean ignored him and raced toward the object—he had to disarm it before anyone could set it off.

"Stop!" That voice came again. "You don't belong here!"

"Neither do you," he answered in the same language. "And if you want to live, you should leave this place."

"Are you mad?" The voice wasn't any closer. "There's nothing here to steal!"

"I am no thief," Sean reached the catwalk that went around the tank—the metallic object was a hundred yards in front of him. "I am only trying to save those aboard this vessel."

"What do you mean?"

"This tank has been rigged to explode," Sean was almost at the device now. "I must stop that from happening."

"Explode?" The voice seemed puzzled. "How could it explode?"

"See this?" Sean had reached the metallic device now. It was duct-taped to the railing. He drew his knife and cut a wire that was attached. "If someone triggers it," he cut it free of the railing and held it up—it was a simple device—just a spark gap, a battery, and a switch. "If it's allowed to spark..." He made a gesture. "This ship—and all aboard—would die in the explosion."

"So that's what they were up to?" The voice was closer now. "I thought it might be something like that!"

"Who are you?" Sean asked, quickly pulling the detonator apart.

"I am Abdul Rachman—ship's engineer."

91

"Happy to meet you, Abdul." Sean turned and saw the man standing just inside the hatch. "Will you accompany me to the bridge?"

"Do you plan to kill me as you did Abdalmalek Farouq?"

"He was the man by the ladder?"

The engineer nodded.

"I had to kill him—if I had not, we would all be dead by now."

"In Paradise with Allah and the seventy-two virgins." The man, who Sean could now tell was older than he'd thought, grinned. "Or seventy-two whatever—the Qu'ran is unclear on that." He shook his head. "The Qu'ran is often unclear—and open to all kinds of interpretations." He gestured to Sean. "Come, I will take you to the bridge."

***

"Piper to Higgins," Farrell jumped as the radio suddenly came to life. "Piper to Higgins—anyone hear me?"

"We have you, Mr. Piper." The radio operator quickly replied.

"Good—I've been inside the ship and the radio does not work from there."

"Roger, we figured that was what happened."

"Good. Please tell the Captain that it's safe to board. The two men responsible for the problem have been neutralized and the rest of the crew is not interested in dying for Allah."

"Boarding party away," the Captain murmured into his microphone. "Weapons on safe, please."

92

"Sean," Farrell stepped up alongside the mike. "Are you sure it's safe?"

"It's safe, Frank. They had a total of three detonators in place and I've taken care of all of them." He paused for a moment. "I also got their computers intact and it looks as if we might have another problem."

"What?"

"I'd rather not put it out over an insecure line—I'll fill you in when you come aboard."

"Okay," Farrell nodded. "I'll be along as soon as I can."

"Take your time," Sean chuckled. "There's no need to rush..."

***

By the time Farrell was able to get aboard, the tanker had been completely occupied by American sailors—although a glance at the crew indicated that they weren't going to have any trouble."

"Hey Frank," Sean looked remarkably chipper. "This is Abdul Rachman—once the engineer of this fine vessel, now, unless I have misread the rules of salvage, her master."

"Mr. Rachman," Farrell took the man's proffered hand. "I'm glad you aren't set on blowing us all to atoms."

"That is not the way of the prophet," the older man said, face serious. "Men like Abdalmalek and his partner dishonor all of us with their continual attempts to hurt others." He shook his head. "Islam is—or should be—a religion of peace!"

93

"So I keep hearing," Farrell sighed. "Mostly from people who are trying to kill me."

"Abdul won't be doing that," Sean put in. "He's gotten the crew in hand—they were actually a bit shocked to find out they were going to be sacrificing their lives on this 'mission'."

"We were all quite surprised," Abdul Rachman smiled. "It wasn't what we signed up for."

"I'm glad we could be of service," Farrell said, still puzzled. "Sean, you had something to show me?"

"Yeah," he turned toward a door at the rear of the bridge. "This way..."

The door led to a short passageway with cabins on both sides.

"This is officer country," Sean told his partner. "The Captain's cabin is closest to the bridge, then comes the first officer, second officer, and so on." He looked at Farrell. "The Abqaiq sailed with only two officers—men named Abdalmalek Farouq and Mansur Al-Enezi—I'm sure we'll find both names on various lists if we look."

"So they were behind this?"

"I don't think so," Sean opened the first door to his right. "This was Abdalmalek cabin—I gather that he was the senior of the two terrorists." He led Farrell to a desk on one side of the room. "This laptop contains, among other things, a full breakdown on how to prepare the tanker for maximum explosive potential and directions on just where to blow it once it reaches the canal."

"So?"

"Somebody was controlling these two— someone who planned this in great detail."

"Again, so?"

"So this same planner has several other tankers at sea right now—and one of them will be reaching New York harbor in about twelve hours!"

***

This time they used the Higgins helicopter to take them directly to the nearest US base—the Ranger training facility in the Canal Zone. From there they took military transport directly to Washington D.C.

They arrived just before dark.

"...So that's the story, Ma'am." Sean took a look around the room. He recognized many of the faces but a few—including that of the FBI representative—were new to him. "We eliminated the threat to the Canal Zone but it appears that there are several more such tankers already at sea—at least one will be in position to accomplish its mission sometime tomorrow afternoon."

"Do we have any idea where these ships came from or who they belong to?" That from the CIA rep in the room—a man who had worked with Sean and Farrell on the Ramnarain case.

"So far I've found four possibilities—all have been reported missing in the last two years and all were written off by the insurance companies that covered them." He tapped a command into his laptop. "I believe that these two ships, at least, are an immediate threat."

A satellite image appeared on the big screen above the briefing table. It showed the Atlantic coast of the US. As the people around the table watched, the image zoomed closer and markers appeared over two vessels.

"The ship marked 'target one' set sail from the Philippines almost three weeks ago—its transponder says it's registered to that country—but they have no record of it."

The imaging on the screen moved again.

"This ship— 'target two'—has a transponder code from Belgium—but again, there is no record of it in Belgian maritime records."

"Can't we check her when she picks up tugboats?"

"No," Sean shook his head. "By that time, she'd be in far enough that a detonation would kill a huge number of people living on both sides of the river."

The Naval officer snorted: "So we send a Destroyer out to intercept them in deep water and see if they're who they say they are."

"I don't think there's time for that," Sean tapped keys again and the screen image changed again. "Both targets will be close to shore by then—one will be in the Hudson by two tomorrow afternoon, the other will be within five miles of the Oil refineries in New Jersey around the same time." He looked at the faces around the table. "And I can't find a single US Naval vessel closer than Norfolk."

"We'll use planes!" The Naval Officer put up his hands."

"And do what? Sink her?" Sean shook his head. "What if I'm wrong? What if she's really what she says she is?"

"Mr. Piper is right." Mary Max' voice was soft but everyone turned her way. "We can't just destroy shipping on hunches and unsubstantiated intel," she looked around the table. "We need to board those ships and find out if they're as dangerous as we think."

"But if we have no assets in the area..."

"Mr. Piper, alone and without back-up, boarded the Abqaiq by dropping from a helicopter." Mary Max raised an eyebrow. "Don't tell me we don't have a SEAL or Ranger team that can't reach these two and do the same."

"We can get a SEAL team on target two in six hours," the Naval officer answered, nodding. "Target One, however, might be too far North..."

"I believe there're a few SEAL's cooling their heels just a few miles from here—waiting for a new assignment from the Pentagon." the Army Colonel who had been silent up to now put in, smiling. "I'm sure they'll be happy to have something to do while they wait."

"Good enough," Mary Max looked around the table. "Mr. Piper will accompany the team going after Target One, Mr. Farrell will handle Target Two." Her eyebrow raised even higher. "Any questions?" She looked around. "No?" She rose to her feet. "Then let's get this show on the road—we don't have too much time."

CHAPTER ELEVEN

It took a few hours and stops at two rather ratty-looking bars but Sean finally found the last of the SEAL's that he'd picked to accompany him on the mission. He briefed them in a hanger on Edwards Air Force Base, made sure they got enough coffee and oxygen to sober up, then led them to the pair of CH-53E Super Stallions that Mary Max had arranged to be flown up from North Carolina.

"Everybody clear on what we have to do?" Sean asked, checking the straps that held his gear in place.

"Seems simple enough," WO2 Michael T. Mize, senior man of those Sean had chosen, tugged on one of his own straps, buckling it tight. "We drop on this tanker and secure it."

"It's got to be quick," Sean pulled the last strap tight. "On the Abqaiq, there were three ways to detonate the tanks—one on the bridge, one in the head man's cabin, and one in the tank itself." He looked Mize in the eyes. "If anyone gets to any of those switches..." He spread his hands. "It's game over for us."

"We understand," the young warrant looked at the three other men of his little group. "Isn't that right, men?"

"Sure is," one of them said, smiling. "Drop on them from above and cut their throats before they can react."

"Let's try not to cut any throats until *after* we're sure we have the right target—all right?"

"You're the boss," Mize smiled. "Although you seem to be a little young for the job."

"My father was a Ranger in the sandbox—you want me to show you how he brought me up?"

The Sergeant shook his head. "No need—I'll see what you have on the mission."

"Good enough," Sean adjusted the sling holding his M-4. "Anyone got any questions?"

The four men were silent.

"All right," Sean gestured to the further of the two helicopters. "who's giving cover?"

"That'd be me." A tall and very skinny buck sergeant raised a hand.

"Beaumont's the best shot I've ever seen," Mize put in. "He can hit anything he sees."

"I hope he can hit it from a moving platform," Sean smiled. "Okay, let's mount up and let's get this done."

A moment later both helicopters were airborne and heading out to sea.

***

"You have gotten no messages?" Muhammed el Arish glared at his companion.

"There is nothing," Ahmed Saal stared at the screen of his laptop. "No reports showing an attack on any of the Infidel targets."

"Abdalmalek should have reached his target by now." The slender man bit his lower lip. "Something must have happened to him." He

99

looked down at Ahmed. "You're sure there's nothing?"

"We are less than one hundred miles from their communications hub—do you not think we would have picked up something about the attack by now?"

"You're right," Muhammed nodded once. "Perhaps he was delayed by bad weather." A slow smile spread across his face. "It gives us the honor of striking first! Has the crew been prepared?"

"I have two men on guard at the fantail—they are armed and ready if anyone tries to board us."

"And the bow?"

"Two men there as well," Ahmed looked at his companion. "It only leaves us four men in reserve. Perhaps we should have brought a larger crew..."

"It was difficult enough to get the men we did." Muhammed shook his head. "Men of the desert do not take easily to the sea."

"I suppose you're right."

"Besides, it does not matter. The Infidel can have no idea of our plans—and the first they will know of them is when we destroy the heart of their accursed New York City!"

The two men both nodded at the thought before returning to their chores. The target was close and neither wanted anything to go wrong now...

***

"That's gotta be the target," Sean pointed to a tanker nearly identical to the Abqaiq just ahead of them. He nudged the pilot. "Tell Chopper two to make their pass."

It had been decided to use the second chopper as a decoy, flying it low over the tanker and, hopefully, drawing all eyes toward it as Sean's own helicopter swooped in low enough for the Rangers to repel down to the deck.

"Everyone ready?" Sean hooked his standard rescue carabiner to one of the ropes and stepped into position.

"Right with you, Boss." Mize took a spot to his left.

"We'll go first, you two," Sean nodded at the others. "Follow as soon as we're clear."

"Roger that," Sgt. Miller answered, holding his thumb up. "We'll be right behind you."

"Good," Sean pulled the big door open. "Let's hope we can get to the triggers in time."

***

Muhammed el Arish frowned as he heard the sound of helicopter rotors. "What is that?" He stepped to the front of the bridge and peered out the big windshield there.

"It looks like an American helicopter." Ahmed shrugged. "Probably their Coast Guard checking the traffic."

"Let us hope that is all it is." The tall man glanced at the trigger behind him. "We need to be further up the river if we are to accomplish our mission."

"Don't worry, this means nothing. I have been here before and always there are many ships and airplanes in the area," he pointed to one side. "See? There're three other ships entering the river right

101

along with us—there is no reason for the Infidels to see us as a threat."

"I hope you're right." Muhammed el Arish ran a hand through his beard. "Although I still worry that we have not heard any word of Abdalmalek's mission."

"Be of good cheer, my friend." Ahmed slapped the taller man on the shoulder. "We are in the hands of Allah—and as we are his servants, what could possibly go wrong?"

***

Sean knew that the ship below was their target as soon as he saw the armed guards fore and aft.

"Weapons free, everyone!" He sent over the team push. "Go in hot!"

He waited a split instant for an acknowledgement then pushed off from the copter and began the quickest descent he could manage.

Mize was right alongside.

"We've got to get to the bridge as quickly as we can!" He winced as he heard a gunshot forward. "If they get to the trigger before we do..."

Sean saw the gunman react to the shot—and look up at the chopper behind him—and the men hanging from a rope beneath it.

"Crap!"

The man's AK-47 came up, pointed at Sean...

"Watch yourself!" He motioned to Mize as tracers began to whiz through the air between them.

I have to get down now! Sean told himself. *Before he gets the range!*

102

He took a split second to judge his height and distance—then hit the quick release on his rappelling gear—and dropped toward the sea below...

The drop seemed to go on forever—then Sean hit the deck of the tanker—hard.

He grunted and used his momentum to roll forward—toward the gunman—and came to his feet with his sidearm drawn and ready.

He fired two shots—and the man went down a split second before Mize reached the deck and deployed his rifle.

"Hell of a move, kid." The Sergeant muttered. "You okay?"

Sean stood up and did a quick check. "Nothing broken," he flexed his legs. "I seem to be in one piece."

"You're a lucky son-of-a-bitch! You could have ended up in the water!"

"I figured I had the momentum to make it—and I didn't want to wait for that bastard," he nodded toward the dead gunman. "To hit something."

"Well, you certainly managed that." Mize shook his head. "Nice shot by the way."

"Thanks," Sean holstered his pistol and pulled his M-4 into position. "But let's talk about this later—I want to get to the bridge before whoever's there can blow this thing from under us."

"I'm with you." He glanced at the chopper where two more men were working their way down and tapped his earbud. "Muller! You and Ransom go belowdecks and check the tanks—rip out anything that looks like trouble!"

"Got it, Boss!" One of them answered.

"Try not to shoot," Sean added. "That might be enough to set the whole thing off."

"Roger that—knives only."

"Good enough," Sean clicked the safety on his M-4 to 'OFF'. "Let's get to it!" He motioned for Mize to follow him and moved swiftly toward the bridge.

"I'll get the door open," Sean said a few moments later when the rear of the Bridge came into sight. "You take out whoever's in there!"

"How about I take the door," the ranger's tone was dry. "I weigh more than you do and I think you already got your share of bruises."

"All right," the bridge hatch was less than thirty feet away. "Let's do it!"

The ranger nodded and sped up until, from less than three feet away, he threw himself, shoulder first, at the door.

Hinges flying, it collapsed inward, revealing two shocked-looking men.

***

"That is definitely gunfire!" Muhammed el Arish gnashed his teeth as he saw the helicopter hovering in front of the tanker, gunfire coming from the open door. "We are discovered!"

"We are almost in position," Ahmed told him. "Just a few more minutes."

"And if they board us?" The taller man shook his head. "No, we must not take the chance!" He turned toward one side of the bridge where a simple switch had been mounted on a chart table. "We cannot fail—not when we are so close!"

"But if we detonate here..." Farouq gestured at the open water around them. "We will do no real damage!"

"How long can we delay?" Muhammed bit his lip. "How much time until the Americans are aboard and in position to stop us?"

"It will be several minutes yet," Farouq gestured to the helicopter forward, still hovering in the same position. "Look, they have put no men on our deck—Amad is still exchanging fire with them—he will hold them off long enough for us to reach our target area."

"Perhaps you are right." Muhammed stopped in front of the switch. "But I will stay here, ready to act, just in case..."

"That is well, my friend. But there is no danger..."

Both men reacted in shock as the hatch suddenly exploded inward in a rain of hinges and screws.

***

Mize slammed into the door with all his weight—and was far more successful than he had anticipated. His impact shattered the hinges and lock sending him and the door flying into the room.

Sean, a step behind, tripped over the flailing legs of the Ranger, sliding helplessly to one side. He could see two men staring at him in shock.

One of them was standing right next to what had to be a switch.

The world stopped. Sean fought to clear his rifle, turning it toward that man. It seemed to take forever—as if he were moving through tar…

As Sean fought with his weapon, the man by the switch shook his head, clearing it, and started to push down on the switch...

Just as a tiny hole appeared in the big front window of the bridge.

The Arab's head exploded before he could finish his move and he slumped backwards—away from the switch.

The other man began to move—but Sean had control of his weapon now and he quickly put a round into the man's knee, dropping him to the ground where, a moment later, he was rendered unconscious by Sean's rifle butt.

"That was exciting," Mize said as he got to his feet. "We're still here so I guess the others took care of business below."

"You were right about Beaumont," Sean sighed as he pushed himself upright. "That was a hell of a shot from a moving platform."

"I'll tell him you said so." Mize went to the switch and, using duct tape, rendered it useless. "What now?"

"We check the cabins for more switches—then we wait for a tug to come alongside." Sean looked around the cabin. "I told Mary Max that the best thing to do with this ship was to sink it in deep water—if we try to vent, we might produce a spark and..." He shrugged.

"Seems like a plan," Mize nodded toward the interior passageway. "Shall we get to it?"

"One moment." Sean produced a plastic riot cuff which he used to bind the still-breathing terrorist. "Okay, let's go." He smiled. "The next door we need to rush to open is mine!"

***

The cleanup went quickly. Muller and Ransom had disarmed the triggering device in the main tank before methodically rounding up the remaining crew members. By the time the Coast Guard (called by the helicopter pilot once the all-clear had been sent) arrived, the ship was completely secure.

"Any word on my partner's operation?" Sean asked as he climbed aboard the launch sent to bring him to shore.

"Sorry sir," the young Ensign operating the vessel shook his head. "I haven't been told anything other than to get you ashore as quickly as possible." He nodded to the two still orbiting helicopters. "They're going to meet us at the nearest landing site," he pointed. "Which is over there on the Jersey side."

"That doesn't sound good," Sean said to Mize as the boat pushed off. "Mary Max wants me back in a hurray—and that can't be a good sign."

"It might be nothing." The Ranger shrugged. "Maybe she just wants a quick debrief."

"I won't be ready for a debrief until I check this laptop," he held up the device he'd found in one of the leader's rooms. "And even then I'm going to want time to question the surviving terrorist."

"I hadn't thought about all that," Mize spread his hands. "This really isn't my field of expertise."

"You do pretty good in your own field," Sean clapped him on the back. "I hope you're going to be around for a bit—I might need you again."

"Anytime." Mize smiled. "You do pretty good work yourself." The smile widened. "For a kid!"

The two chuckled and settled back for the ride to shore.

CHAPTER TWELVE

Sean studied the captured laptop during the ride back to DC. Some of it was in languages he didn't know, which meant he'd have to use translation programs to figure them out.

He had them in his own computer so he figured to get to work as soon as he landed.

He changed his mind when he saw Mary Max waiting at the FBI helipad.

"He's all right, Sean." She told him before he could ask any questions. "He was far enough away from the blast to survive."

"Survive?" He shook his head. "What happened?"

"He used pretty much the same tactic you did— sending one chopper over the tanker while he approached from the rear."

"And?"

"Whoever was on the bridge detonated as soon as the first helicopter turned and began orbiting." She shook her head. "The blast radius was nearly double your estimate."

"More fuel, more air, bigger radius." Sean's voice was numb. "What happened to the two choppers?"

"The trailing helicopter—that was the one Frank was on--was badly damaged in the explosion. It was forced to autorotate and barely made it to dry land." She shook her head. "The landing was kind of rough."

"The other helicopter?"

Her face went blank. "They didn't make it."

Sean sighed. "Any casualties on shore?"

"None found so far." She looked at him. "It would have been had if the ship had gotten any closer—you saved a lot of lives."

"Lost some, too."

"You should get some rest."

"There's no time," he held up the captured laptop. "I have to see what I can glean from this thing." He looked at her. "And we took a prisoner—it would be nice to be able to interrogate him."

"I'll get him shipped here." She looked at him, worry in her eyes. "Do you need anything else?"

"Keep Mize and his SEAL team around—we might need them again."

"Easy enough."

"Good," he took a step forward. "I'll get to work on this—I need to translate some things before I'm sure what it says."

"When will you know?"

"Give me four hours."

"I'll set up a briefing then."

"And make sure we have a track on those other ships I identified—we need to know where they are."

"Already done—and the Navy is moving assets to have some units in position if needed."

"Good," Sean rubbed the back of his hand across his face. "I'll see you in four hours." He strode off, then stopped and turned back toward her. "And could you please make sure that the Rangers get a nice meal? They did a very professional job."

"Of course." She nodded. "We'll take care of them."

"Good," Sean turned back toward the building and his office—time, he knew, was of the essence now.

***

Hamid el Raacqi smiled as he watched the sea roll by. The voyage had been far smoother than he had expected and now, finally, he was within striking distance of his destination.

"That is the Infidel's 'Bridge Tunnel' ahead," his companion on this quest, Sidig Adib, gestured to the span that filled the window in front of them. "We are close to our destination."

"How close?" Hamid asked.

"Perhaps three hours, perhaps a bit more." Sidig shrugged. "Does it really matter now?"

"The Infidels might still locate us."

"Impossible!" Sidig shook his head. "Our transponder is switched off and we have not requested a pilot." He stroked his beard. "they will only realize who we are when they are surrounded by fire!"

"I hope you are right, my friend." Hamid tapped his laptop. "There is no evidence that any of the others have succeeded."

"Perhaps they were not worthy of their tasks." The rather rotund Sidig raised his hands eloquently. "Unlike the two of us!"

"Allah grant you are right." The slimmer Hamid answered. "For we are certainly in his hands..."

"There are two more," Sean said as he seated himself in the now-crowded briefing room.

"Two?" There was a new Naval Officer now—with a higher rank. "Are you sure?"

"I'm sure." Sean took a deep breath. "All of these ships are working on a plan put forward by a CIA consultant nearly ten years ago. I haven't been able to figure how they got the plans yet, but they're definitely using them."

"You haven't had the time," Mary Max put in. "You've been on the go since your original discovery."

"I guess." Sean touched the keyboard on his laptop and images appeared on the big screen behind him. "Last time I was in here, I told you I suspected four ships," shapes were highlighted on the screen. "We neutralized two." Two of the shapes disappeared. "But these two are still moving toward their targets and one of them," he circled it in red. "Is very close—perhaps too close—right now."

"Where is that?" The Naval Officer leaned forward.

"That is Norfolk Virginia—the largest Naval base on the East Coast."

"Shit," he bit his lip, then: "Give me the data and I'll get a destroyer out there to intercept immediately."

"Here," Sean slid a flash drive across the table. "I was hoping you could deal with this one."

"I'll let you know," the officer stood and left the room.

"Now, the other target," Sean circled it in yellow, "is out here in the Atlantic." He spread his hands. "I'm not sure of the target—it could be any number of places along the coast."

"Are you sure it's held by terrorists."

"Sure as I can be without more information." Sean ran a hand over his forehead. "It certainly fits the profile of all the others." He looked at Mary Max. "I'd like to take the helicopters and the Rangers and go take a look."

"I'd rather you got some sleep," she looked at him. "But you're not going to do that, are you?"

She didn't wait for an answer.

"All right, I'll set things up. You get some food—I'll meet you in the canteen when I have everything you'll need."

"Thank you, Ma'am." Sean hesitated. "The prisoner we took..."

"Is being patched up now—he'll be in custody here by the time you get back."

"Thank you, Ma'am." Sean smiled. "I guess I could use some food..."

***

"Hey Sean," Mize greeted the young agent as he entered the canteen. "Anything?"

"I thought you guys were going to have a meal? Somewhere nice?"

"Your boss offered a place," Mize gestured. "We decided to stay here—the chow's fine and

113

we're handy if you need us." He smiled. "Do you need us?"

"Probably." Sean grabbed a tray, loaded up with enough food for two normal men. "The computer says we have one more target, if I can't figure another way…"

"Then we hit it." Mize nodded. "Good enough for me, we'll hang around."

"Shouldn't be long," Sean started eating. "Mary Max will bring the details to me here when we're ready."

"Good," Mize smiled. "We'll get some coffee."

"You know," Sgt Miller added. "You have enough food for two there."

"Yeah," Sean took another bite. "I have a quick metabolism—really quick."

"I'll take your word for it." Miller smiled.

They settled in to wait.

***

Samir Jalil looked gloomily out of the forward viewscreen of his vessel. The other ships had failed to report—that was bad. Worse because all of them should have been in range before now.

"They have failed," Abd Al Jabbar said as he entered the bridge. "All of them."

"Perhaps they have been delayed by weather." Jalil answered.

"All of them?" Al Jabbar shook his head. "No. They have been detected and destroyed."

"Our mission remains the same," Jalil stated. "We must maneuver into port and set off our tank."

114

"Indeed." Al Jabbar nodded. "But which port?" He moved closer to the window, looking out at darkness. "Where can we do the most damage?"

"We can do the most damage to New York," Jalil said. "But I believe we should go to Washington D.C."

"The heart of the infidel!"

"Indeed." He stood up. "We can be there sometime tomorrow…"

"Then let us do it." Al Jabbar said. "Before the weather does us a disservice."

"Allah willing," Jalil said. "We will." He turned to the controls of the ship, made an adjustment.

"It is done." The ships engines speeded up. "Allah grant us speed."

"If he does not," Al Jabbar noted. "Let all our guns be ready for any problem at all."

***

Back in D.C., Sean finished the last of his meal and stood up as Mary Max entered the room.

"I did a full workup, as you suggested." She said. "The boat on the way to Norfolk has picked up a Naval unit, they've been ordered to stand to."

"We'd better warn them not to get too close!"

"We have, they're standing off and using their guns to back up the order." She smiled. "We should know any minute."

"Good," Sean looked at her. "How about the other ship?"

"We have nothing near enough to stop her, and no satellites that have a view—we don't know."

"We've got to find out." His eyebrows went up. "Our prisoner, perhaps?"

"He'll be here in a few minutes," Mary Max told Sean. "We'll have him in an observation room."

"Good," Sean nodded. "I want to speak to him—and I want my friends here to stay ready until I do."

"I think we can handle that." She smiled. "Upstairs is happy enough to allow us to do the dirty work on this one."

"Good," he started for the door. "Let's get it done."

***

Ahmed stood in the interrogation chamber, staring at the door. He knew he had been captured, knew that his ship was no longer a threat.

Allah had abandoned him.

The door opened.

"So," Sean looked over the standing Arab. "You're looking a bit better." He stepped to the side of that table, sat down. "Have a seat," he gestured.

Ahmed stared at him. This was the American who had shattered his dreams! The one who had come through that shattered doorway, rifle ready.

The one who had captured him.

"I will tell you nothing!" He stated, distancing himself from the infidel.

Sean shrugged. "I don't care," he tapped a device in his hand. "As you can see from this map…"

116

A projector put the map on the back wall of the room. It showed the ships of the Arab fleet, spread out across the ocean.

"We know of your plans," Sean maneuvered his device. "These ships," four of the vessels vanished from the screen. "Have already been neutralized." He pointed again. "This one..." A marker appeared over the Norfolk ship. "Is being met by two US Navy Destroyers." He smiled. "That leaves only this single ship." He highlighted the vessel far out in the ocean. "To do us any harm." He smiled at Ahmed. "Of course, we will deal with it before it gets much closer."

The Arab's head spun. *He knew so much!* It was impossible.

"So," Sean stared at the Arab. "Tell me who is manning these ships." He leaned closer. "I can save them from your stupid Jihad."

Ahmed looked at Sean. "Our Jihad is lawful and respectable—you infidels..."

"Are going to destroy your ships and kill your men if you don't tell us what we need to know." Sean looked at the screen. "And you don't have long to do it."

"NO!" Ahmed flung himself against the chains holding him. "I will not!'

"Your call," Sean told him calmly. "You can rot in your cell while we finish the last of your countrymen." Sean stood and moved to the door. "I hope it helps you sleep."

The door slammed behind him.

***

117

"No luck, Mary Max." Sean sighed. "We'll have to destroy the Norfolk ship immediately."

Mary Max nodded. "The Navy's got that covered."

"And me and the SEAL's will have to visit the second ship." He looked at her. "And make sure it's a danger before we destroy it."

"Don't take too many chances." She told him. "Use the SEAL's first—that's what they're trained for."

Sean nodded.

"And Sean," she gave him a hard look. "Don't go hang-gliding in like you did last time—prisoners don't do us any good if you end up dead."

"I get it." Sean nodded again. "I'll be careful."

"You be more than that," Mary Max made her look harder still. "You come back unharmed—hear me?"

"I get you, Ma'am." Sean threw off a salute. "I'll be back."

With that he turned and hurried off.

***

"We are within an hour of reaching the neck of the river," Jalil said. "I have gotten the most speed I can from the engines."

"Allah hide us from our enemies," Al Jabbar put in. "I only hope the sky stays dim and gray," he looked up. "To prevent their seeing us from their accursed satellites."

"Ins Allah." Jalil answered.

"Indeed," Al Jabbar nodded. "It is in the hands of Allah—may he be merciful."

***

At that same moment, the two CH-53E choppers were less than ten miles away. They had reached the projected point where the ship was supposed to have been and found no sign.

Now they were flying a circular course to locate it.

"It can't be too far," Sean stared at the ocean with his binoculars. "It must have turned since our satellite saw it last."

"Over there!" Mize gestured. "About 100 degrees off our bow."

Sean hurried over and looked—the ship was there, steaming hard for the American coast.

"That's her," Sean studied the ship. "She's heading for the coast all right." He looked up. "I can't see where she's going, though."

"She's heading for the Potomac." Mize let his glasses slide down on his chest. "If she's light enough, she might be able to run up it to…"

"Washington!" Sean glanced at it again. "We'll have to go aboard and stop it—alert your men."

"Right," Mize looked at Sean. "And us first this time, okay?"

Sean nodded slowly. "Yeah, it's what Mary Max wants this time…"

The Chopper speeded up and turned toward the ship.

***

"Captain!" The seaman was yelling as he approached the bridge. "We have helicopters coming our way!"

"They have found us." Jalil stated flatly. "We must fight them off!"

"Wait!" Al Jabbar held up a hand. "They may just be surveying us—keep the guns hidden until we are sure!"

"You may be right...they could be Coast Guard..." He stood up. "It does not matter! We are too close!" He turned to the men and began issuing orders. "All hands! Man your guns—and hold your fire until I give the word!" He looked at the two choppers as they approached. "Let us give them time to get nice and close..."

***

"Lines ready?" Sean looked, saw the men holding the ropes at the door. "Get ready..." He looked out...

And the ship opened fire.

"Damn!" Sean ducked back inside. "That ships got all kinds of weapons!"

"We've got to pull back," Mize told him. "Gotta get prepared."

"No," Sean touched his chin, thinking. "We don't have time—it'll be in the Potomac in minutes?"

"What do you have in mind?"

"Captain!" Sean leaned toward the pilot. "Bear in on that ship," he looked down. "Get us aboard—any way you can."

"Roger," the pilot replied. "Hang on!"

The ship made a sudden lunge to the left, tossing Sean against the bulkhead. He was just recovering when...

"We're hit!" Mize yelled. "The tail!"

"Everybody get ready," Sean ordered, standing up. "We're going aboard!"

The chopper shuddered—and limped toward the ship.

***

"Damn!" Al Jabbar cursed loudly. "That helicopter is coming!"

"We will shoot it down," Jalil said. "It has no chance!"

"Chance or not," Al Jabbar looked out the window. "Here it comes!"

There was a chorus of curses from the crewman manning the weapons as both helicopters returned fire—then sudden silence.

"They got our machine gunners!" Al Jabbar cursed again. "They will be here soon!"

"Too late!" Jalil held up an arm. "Duck!"

The helicopter crashed onto the deck, the rotors slamming into the pilot house.

***

"Move! Move! Move" Mize was yelling as he bailed out of the crashing chopper. "Get to the bridge!

Sean watched his companions jump down onto the deck. They swarmed over the ship, firing at the crewman.

121

Men fell.

I've got to get to the bridge, Sean thought. *There's no time…*

A bullet whizzed by, close enough that it rustled the fabric of his jacket.

Close! He jumped onto the deck. *But not close enough…*

He fired at a crewman, ducking behind an air vent. *They're all firing!* He looked ahead. *Where is the bridge…*

He spotted the pilot house.

Gotta get there fast! He got a foot under his body and leaped forward. "Come on! The Pilot House is up there!" He fired from the hip, emptying his rifle. "Come on!"

Mize and his men moved, firing as they went.

***

"They will be here any second!" Jalil said. "What should we do?"

"We cannot let them take the ship," Al Jabbar looked at him. "Ignite the fuse!"

"But the men…"

"Are in the arms of Allah." He looked at Al Jabbar. "Do it!"

"Ins Allah," Jalil said, nodding. "I will…"

Then he dropped to the deck boneless, hit by a stray as Sean and Mize came through the door, firing as they moved.

"NO!" Al Jabbar stood up, brandished a pistol. "I will …!"

Mize shot him dead before he could aim the weapon.

122

"That's one of them," he yelled. "And the other?"

Sean stepped past him, bent over the body of Jalil. "Still alive." He looked at Mize. "Check on the men, and get us a medic for this guy." Sean shook his head. "He's been hit but he's a long way from being dead."

***

"We've got three dead," Mize reported a few minutes later. "Should have more but we got lucky," he spat on the floor. "They just sprayed and prayed."

Sean nodded. "Prisoners?"

"Twenty-three," Mize smiled. "Most of them are wounded."

"Good enough," Sean nodded again. "I've called for help. The Coast Guard is on the way."

"In the meantime," Mize told him. "We've disarmed all the triggers in the fuel area—and there were a bunch."

"We were lucky," Sean sighed. "They weren't ready for this kind of confrontation, had they been…"

"Yeah, it woulda been bad."

"How's the second chopper?"

"Still in the air," Mize looked at Sean. "You got a reason for asking?"

"Yeah," Sean looked at him. "I'm thinking of going back with our prisoner. I think he knows a lot and these files," he pointed to a box of paperwork. "Have a lot of secrets to tell us."

123

"Okay," Mize nodded. "I'll signal the chopper to pick you up."

"Pick us up," Sean said. "You, me, and our prisoner." He stood up. "Leave Miller in command."

"Miller got hit, I'll leave Starkey."

Sean frowned. "Miller get hit badly?"

"He's dead." Mize stood up. "Caught a bullet in the head."

"That's too bad. I…"

"It's the job." He turned to the door. "Don't let it bother you." He went through. "He's my burden."

Sean nodded and gathered up the paperwork, it suggested something and he was determined to discover what it was.

***

"This suggests they have a base—a place to set up these attack ships." Sean was hunched over the pile of paper he's gotten on the ship. "They may have three or four more ready to go right now! We've got to do something about it."

"Sean," Mary Max stood in the doorway of his office. "I understand the problem. What is the solution again?"

"We have to go there, smash this base." He looked at her. "It's the only way that's safe."

"And where is the base?"

"Persian Gulf, right about…" He took out a map. "Here."

He pointed at a spot on the left side of the Gulf of Bushehr.

"That's in Iran, is it not?"

"Yeah, so..." He turned to her. "We can't touch it, can we."

"Not at the moment." Mary Max smiled at him. "So, take some time off—get some food." She raised an eyebrow. "Relax."

"But the base..."

"Will still be there when you get back." She shooed him. "Go. Get out of here."

"Well, okay." He stood up. "But we need to get that base—it's a constant danger..."

"Think about it—we'll find a way—LATER." She stared at him. "Get lost for a couple of days— I'm serious now, I don't want to see you at all this week."

"All right," he felt a smile tug at his face. "I guess I could go visit Connie..."

"Go, visit your girlfriend." Mary Max smiled back. "I'll work on this, maybe have an answer in a week or so." She looked at him. "Now get out of here!"

He left, grudgingly.

CHAPTER THIRTEEN

Connie, it turned out, had a day off coming. Sean had appeared, as if from nowhere, and asked her out—and she was more than willing. They spent the day driving around, checking out bookstores and the like, ending up in Orlando where they had a very nice meal.

Sean could have treated Connie like a pickup—but he didn't, he treated her like a lady—and she responded in the same way.

The day ended with desert and coffee. Sean did not go into Connie's apartment, although he could have tried.

He was back in Washington the next day.

"What's new," he asked Mary Max as he came into the office.

"Your captive gave us a little info," she answered. "It appears that the remnants of several terrorist groups have banded together. They've 'liberated' a number of small tankers and have devoted their landing area to rework them as suicide craft." She looked at him. "They still have a number of ships in progress."

"How many?"

"We'll know sometime tonight." She looked at a clock. "Our dedicated satellite passes over at seven."

"And then?"

"That hasn't been decided." She turned away from him. "Some of the civilian agencies want to leave them alone—after all, they are in Iran…"

"That's crazy! Those ships will be coming our way and we can't expect to find all of them in time. We have to stop them at the source!"

"Which is why you, and SEAL team three, will embark with *Theodore Roosevelt* tomorrow." She turned back. "It will take several days to get there—I assume you'll bring along something to do during that time."

"Yeah," Sean nodded his head. "I'll find something…"

"Good." Mary Max checked her watch. "Arrange things with Mr. Farrell, he'll be home later this afternoon and," she looked into his eyes. "Good luck, Mr. Piper."

He nodded and left the office, thinking about what needed to be done in the next few hours."

***

"So," he told Farrell a few hours later. "I spent the weekend with my friend Connie down in Florida," he smiled. "We had a really good time."

"Did you make out with her?"

"No," Sean shrugged. "Didn't seem the right thing to do at this point in the relationship."

Farrell shook his head. "You could be dead before you get down there again—you should have just…"

"Mr. Farrell, Mr. Piper," Mary Max stuck her head in the door. "Come to the briefing room, please."

"Of course, Ma'am." Sean said, standing up. "C'mon," he took Farrell's shoulder. "Let's see what this is all about."

127

"You're about to lose a couple of fingers if you don't lay off," Farrell snarled. "I'm still sore in that area."

"Sorry." Sean let go, headed for the door.

"Forget it," Farrell tried to catch up. "And slow down, damn it!"

They reached the briefing room together, walking in as people stared to sit down.

"These are my experts," Mary Max intoned. "Mr. Piper and Mr. Farrell." She pointed to seats. "If you would."

Sean and Farrell both gave her a quick nod and sat.

"Mr. Piper has led the attacks on the ships we've caught thus far." She nodded at Sean. "He will be the leader of the expedition going out tomorrow."

"Isn't he kind of young?" the CIA man asked. "I mean…"

"He has my full confidence," Mary Max replied. "And that of the Secretary of Defense."

"Oh," the CIA man nodded. "Well, if the SecDef is okay with him…"

"He is," Mary Max stared at the man. "As is the Secretary of the Navy and the head of FBI." Her gaze seemed to weigh him down. "Is there a question?"

"No Ma'am," the man answered, head down. "None at all."

"Good," Mary Max pushed a button, displaying a map. "Here is the Persian Gulf—as you can see, we have a large number of Naval Vessels in the area."

She pressed another button and the map was reduced. "All of the naval units are stationed in this area," she pointed with a laser. "Offshore by over a hundred miles."

"That's so Iran can't complain," the man from the Naval Secretary's Office explained. "And we still have some firepower handy if it's needed."

There was a general nod, then Mary Max cut in again:

"The terrorists have built a base here," she enlarged the map again, showing the terrorist site near the Gulf of Bashehr." Another button. "Here's the satellite photo from about an hour ago."

They all leaned in. The satellite photo was very clear, having been shot in good weather. It showed the base quite well. There were a number of tankers moored all around and quite a few smaller craft going between them.

"As you can see," Mary Max pointed out. "They have quite a fleet building up—ten or eleven small tankers and two," she pointed again. "Larger ships—Supertankers I think they're called."

"And each one," the CIA man took over for a moment, "Is being set up as a floating bomb."

"The one we took out in Chesapeake was smaller—maybe half that size." The Naval man noted. "It made a huge bang! Good thing it didn't reach its target area."

"Indeed," Mary Max said. "And what if one or more of these do?"

"It would cause panic," the CIA man said. "We couldn't trust anything coming into our ports."

129

"And we can't just destroy a tanker for no reason," the Naval man added. "That would be an act of war!"

"Which is why the *ROOSEVELT* is sailing tomorrow with a SEAL team and our young leader, Mr. Piper." She smiled thinly. "Their job will be to reach the site, leave the Naval vessel, and destroy that base." She turned her gaze on Mr. Piper. "I believe it can be done—and Mr. Piper seems to be the one to do it."

Sean nodded quietly.

***

The ROOSEVELT is a boomer," Farrell told Sean the next morning. "Sixteen nuclear weapons." He looked at the young man. "We'd prefer not to use them."

"I get the plan," Sean nodded. "I take the team in and we blow the place to hell and gone then," he looked at Farrell. "We beat feet back to the ROOSEVELT and come home."

"You think you can do it?"

Sean looked him in the face. "Do you think I can't?"

Farrell shook his head. "I think you can do most anything." He pointed ahead. "There's the Naval Yard."

"Drop me at the gate." Sean told him. "And take care of the office until I get back." He grinned. "You can do that with your bad wing, right?"

"Get going, kid!" Farrell growled. "I'll see you when you get back."

Sean grabbed his kit and headed for the pier. His face was set and ready.

***

"Here's your place, sir." The crewman showed Sean to a bunk in a small stateroom. "I hope it'll do."

"It's fine." Sean said, tossing his bag onto the bad. "Who do I bunk with?"

"Me," Mize smiled as he entered. "Hope that's okay."

"Nice to see you," Sean smiled. "I hoped you'd be with the crew."

"Same guys," Mize nodded. "Except we've got Davis as a replacement for Miller."

"Too bad about Miller, I'm sorry."

"No need." Crews tossed his bag on the other bunk. "The others are ready to go where you go." He smiled. "They think you're lucky with this sort of attack."

"Let's hope they right." Sean stood. "I've got to see the Captain."

"He's on the bridge," Mize grinned. "Waiting for you."

"Okay," Sean headed down the corridor. "See you later."

CHAPTER FOURTEEN

Commander Robert Anson was in a good mood. His sub had cleared the port and was running smoothly toward the ocean. Everything was going well—and now he had the FBI snot to worry about.

"Mr. Piper," he shook hands. "I have some orders about you."

"Nothing too onerous, I hope." Sean replied.

"That's to be seen." He looked at the young agent. "Seems we have to get you and the SEAL's to a place near Iran." He shook his head. "Not friendly territory."

"I know," Sean took a pace to the side to allow a crewman to pass. "I also know you've been in the area before—last cruise, perhaps?"

Anson chuckled. "Maybe so." He shook his head. "Aren't you a little young for this sort of thing?"

"My dad trained me for it from birth," Sean answered. "How old do I have to be?"

"Good answer, Mr. Piper. Good answer." Anson smiled. "We'll be at sea in an hour or so, please contact me if you need anything."

"Anything?"

Anson chuckled again. "Well…"

Sean sketched out a salute. "I'll stay out of the way, Captain." He turned away. "You have my word."

The Captain nodded slowly.

"How're they doing, Ma'am." Farrell asked as he entered the office a few days later.

"Pretty well," Mary Max answered. "The Navy says they're about halfway." She looked at him. "Time to check his info—that's your job."

"I've gone through the same documents he did." Farrell noted. "And I see where he came to the conclusion he did. The only thing…"

"Yes?"

"Ma'am, I can't find a group to assign this too." Farrell looked out the window. "The base is there, I'm sure of that, but…"

"But you think it might just be the Mullahs of Iran." Mary Max looked at him. "I think you might be right—and I think that was the conclusion Sean came to as well." She signed. "His conclusions came out hard and fast," she shook her head. "Too hard and fast. I thought he knew more than he was saying…"

"I can check again," Farrell told her. "Perhaps there's something I missed."

"Go ahead," Mary Max closed her eyes for a moment. "See if there's anything there."

"And if there isn't?"

"If there isn't," she looked at him, eyes showing her pain. "I'm afraid Sean might have bitten off more than he can chew—and we can't do a thing to help him."

At that moment, Sean and Mize were standing on the deck of the *Roosevelt*. It was dark and the sub had surfaced to do some housekeeping.

133

"How far do you think we've come?" Sean asked.

"Looks like about halfway." Mize looked at him quizzically. "What are you so worried about?"

"What makes you think I'm worried."

"Come off it," Mike shook his head. "I know you pretty well after the last couple of jobs—there's something bothering you. Is it the mission?"

"Partially," Sean moved a little further from the bridge. "I told everyone that there was a base being used on the Gulf of Bashehr. There is—but I'm not so sure about the terrorists being the ones using it."

"You think it's the Iranians?"

"I don't want to but…" He turned to look at his friend. "It reads that way."

"I see." Mize took a moment to think about it. "And this was your way to handle it once and for all."

"Yeah," Sean chuckled. "I don't like to play 'whack a mole'."

"And the big boys bought it?"

"CIA was unsure."

"But they went along, right?"

"Yeah, after they got pushed a bit."

Mize shrugged. "So, we destroy an Iranian base instead of a terrorist base—what's the difference?"

"They'll have better defenses."

"Yeah, and…"

"We'll get no support if we're caught."

"Again, so?"

"I just…just wanted you to know what we were doing."

134

"Sean," Mike smiled. "It's all good with me—and my men will feel the same way."

Sean visibly relaxed. "All right." He looked out to sea. "I guess we'll be there in about two more days."

Mike gave him a pat on the shoulder. "And we'll be ready."

***

Two days later, the *Roosevelt* was sitting on the bottom, less than ten miles from the Iranian base.

"Here's our position," the Captain was briefing both Sean and Mike at the same time. "After dark, we'll surface and let you off here," he pointed to the map. "About 2 miles from the coast. You can make it from there?"

"Yes, sir." Mize smiled. "We have two boats aboard; they should make it easy on a trip this short."

"An Iranian patrol goes through this area," another jab at the map. "Every half hour or so—you'll have to avoid her whatever way you can." He looked at Sean. "For your information, that base is active, working to deploy another group of ships—it would be good to have it shut down."

"We'll do our best, skipper." He smiled. "I think we'll get it done all right."

"I do too," he rolled up the map. "Be back at the ship two hours after we let you out—if you miss that rendezvous, we'll surface again one hour later. If you miss then..." He shrugged. "Orders are to write you off and go on patrol as usual."

135

"I guess we'll make it okay." Sean grinned. "Don't worry."

"I'm not worried," he looked at them. "It's your butts on the line." He put the map back. "I guess that's all. Get some sleep—we'll wake you and your crew when it's time."

"Thanks," Sean smiled. "We'll be ready."

***

"They'll be getting off the boat now," Farrell said. "Into the rubber boats SEAL teams use."

"Weather?" Mary Max asked.

"Good," Farrell rubbed his face. "Too good—moons down but visibility is good."

"Let's hope they make it without having to stir things up too much." She smiled. "I'm not ready for an international incident."

"Sean will do his best."

"I know," Mary Max sighed. "I just hope his best is good enough."

***

Back at the *Roosevelt*, the team was loading into two rubber boats. Sean was worried, looking over clear skies and very visible waters—but the captain had told him that it was now or never.

Mike was working with the NCO's to get the SEAL team in place. He planned to man boat two while Sean took boat one.

They were almost ready to shove off.

"I'll see you later, Mr. Piper." The Captain shook hands with the young man. "Good luck."

"Thank you, sir." Sean answered. "It should be quick." He smiled, "we have plenty of C-4."

"So, I understand." The Captain looked out over the sea. "Be careful of their shore patrol—and don't try to do too much." He smiled. "We can spare a missile or two if it becomes necessary."

"Let's hope it doesn't," Sean stepped away. "See you in a few hours." He turned. "Mr. Mize, are you ready?"

Mike, on boat two, nodded quickly. "Ready to go."

"Good," Sean stepped into his boat. "Let's be off."

The two boats suddenly floated free and as the *Roosevelt* sank beneath the calm sea. A moment later, they started to paddle into the terrorist site.

***

"Is that a raft?" Adelran asked, his glasses trained on the water ahead."

"I cannot tell," Gervais answered. "There is not enough light to be sure."

"Guide the boat that way," Adelran ordered. "We will see."

Some distance away, boat two was watching the Iranian craft.

"They're coming our way," Mize noted. "Everyone—into the water."

"But Sarge," Koenig spoke up. "How're we going to handle them from there?"

"Quietly, son." Mize smiled. "Very quietly." He lifted an arm toward boat one. "Keep it going,

Sean. We got the patrol boat." He spoke quietly, knowing his earbud would pick it up.

"Got you, Mike." Sean looked back. "We'll meet you at the target."

"Roger." Mize was in the water now, the boat just a black spot behind him. "See you there."

Sean's men didn't bat an eye. They kept paddling, their objective right in front of them.

"All right," Sean whispered a few minutes later. "Ship oars—we'll start with that craft." He pointed toward a tanker anchored less than fifty yards ahead. "Who's got some C-4 ready?"

Three hands rose. He took the prepared charge from the closest man and leaned forward.

"That's one," he whispered as the charge cemented itself in place. "Let's go there." He pointed to a point where three craft were anchored in a bunch. "Quietly, now…"

Behind him, the Iranian patrol had reached the suspected area. The men aboard looked the area over very carefully. They noticed the floating raft—they didn't notice the men climbing quietly over the stern.

***

Ten minutes later, the second raft floated into the docking area, the SEAL's aboard were very quiet.

"Sean," Mike radioed in a subdued voice. "Where are you, Sean?"

"To your right," Sean's voice was quite clear and sharp. "How'd it go with the patrol boat?"

"Very well," Mike answered quietly. "There're no longer a problem."

"Good," Sean looked around. "You take the ships on the left; we'll continue down the right side."

"Roger," Mize smiled. "We'll get right on it."

"Good," Sean said quietly. "If we're careful, they won't find out we were here until 9AM tomorrow."

He got back to work, letting Mize take the left side.

CHAPTER FIFTEEN

Just before sunrise, the *Roosevelt* came quietly to the surface.

"Be careful, men," the captain told the watch crew. "There's liable to be a watch boat around here—don't let them see us."

"Roger, sir." The portside lookout answered. "We'll be careful." He put the binoculars to his eyes and started scanning the ocean.

The Captain nodded, and settled into position with his own binoculars. They should be re-appearing any time...

"There they are!" The starboard lookout noted. "Two rubber boats." He leaned forward. "I can't tell if there's any problems..."

"Pickup crew to the bridge!" The Captain muttered into his all-ship relay. "Let's get them aboard nice and fast!"

Boat One, with Sean in command, moved quietly into position alongside the sub. The men came aboard, moving quickly and efficiently, helped by the Pickup Crew.

"Get below," Sean ordered. "Don't hold up the ship's crew!"

One by one, the SEAL's obeyed, finding an opening and heading into the heart of the ship until only Sean was on deck.

"Go well?" The Captain asked.

"Mission went fine," Sean answered. "But Boat Two had an encounter with the Iranian Guard ship, I don't know if they lost anyone."

"Your earbud?"

"Cut out when they joined us." Sean shook his head. "I know Mize is okay but aside from that, I don't know a thing."

"They'll be alongside soon," the Captain answered. "Then we'll know."

They both stared at the tiny boat in the distance.

***

"They should be coming back about now," Farrell's eyes never left the console wired into Navy Operations. "We should hear…"

"Be calm, Mr. Farrell." Mary Max looked at him. "We trained the young man, we have to give him time to do the sort of work we've trained him for, do we not?"

"Yes, but…"

A light came on over the big board.

"They've returned to the *Roosevelt*," Mary Max stated calmly. "The captain will take her down quickly." She turned away. "We'll hear nothing for a few hours."

"Did they accomplish the mission?" Farrell shook his head. "Lose any of their men?" He stood up. "When will he contact us so we'll know

"A few hours, Mr. Farrell." Mary Max walked away. "We'll get all the information in a few hours."

She left the office quietly, heading for the garage.

***

141

Sean sat at the chow table silently. Mize was seated right across from him and was talking rapidly.

"We couldn't avoid the patrol ship, so I abandoned—temporarily—the rubber boat and set up an assault."

"And?"

"We took them pretty much by surprise—there were only three of them, the two on the bridge and one in the motor area." Mike looked at Sean. "We took the two on the bridge quickly. The one below deck took a little time."

"Who got hurt."

"Koenig got a cut on his leg—he's in sick bay now, Hickman got a tiny scratch on his hand—not worth the time of the pharmacist's mate…"

"Is that all?"

"Jonas got stabbed," Mike shook his head. "By one of ours—it was an accident…"

"How bad?"

"Well, he won't be playing the fiddle for a few weeks…"

"And that's it?"

"Cross my heart."

"I guess I can make my report to Mary Max, then." He looked at his watch. "Right after our C-4 goes off."

He got up and headed for the bridge.

***

"Satellite's in position," Farrell said. "We've got a pretty good image."

142

"I hope Sean did a good job placing those mines," Mary Max looked at the image. "I see seven vessels there. It would be a bitch trying to shadow all of them."

"I agree, but..."

The screen erupted in flame. Bits of metal and wood flew into the air. When the cloud has passed, the interior of the base was nothing but rubble.

"I guess he placed them right."

"Indeed." Mary Max nodded. "Let the White House know—I'll notify the alphabet agencies."

"Right." Farrell looked at the screen. "It looks as if we can give the boy harder tasks now."

"We can." Mary Max smiled. "And he's nobody's boy."

***

The men on the *Roosevelt* had seen the blast—and knew that it had been set and arranged by their passengers.

It brought a sea change in the way they were treated.

"Nice job, Mr. Piper, sir." One of the officers said later that day. "You really got the job done."

"It was the SEAL's," Sean smiled. "They made it easy."

The officer smiled—and Sean's marks went up another few notches. It never hurt to give credit to the people you work with.

That became obvious when the Captain called Sean the next day.

143

"I've got contact with the world," he told the young man. "And they're pleased by the job you did."

"That's nice," Sean frowned. "Why did you want to see me?"

"I wanted to personally congratulate you." The Captain smiled. "And I've been instructed to tell you that you are ordered," He looked Sean in the eyes. "Ordered to return to D.C. with 'all possible speed'." The look turned harder. "Message came from your boss."

"Oh." Sean nodded slowly. "I see…"

"We'll be coming up on a base is Saudi Arabia in less than a day," the Captain smiled. "I assume you can get a ride home from there."

"Sure, no problem," Sean smiled at the Captain. "Thanks." He drifted away, headed for his 'stateroom' and the privacy there.

***

"What'd he say?" Mize asked as Sean arrived in their stateroom.

"Message came in from Mary Max," he said. "She wants me home as quickly as I can get there—don't know why.

"So, home right away…"

"All possible speed." He looked at Mike. "That sound like a friendly message? It feels wrong to me—a little clipped."

"Sometimes officers do this kind of thing," Mize responded. "It just means that she wasn't sure what would happen and now," he nodded at Sean. "She wants to make sure you get back."

144

"I hope you're right." Sean stared at the ceiling, thinking, then: "I guess I can get a ride in Saudi Arabia …"

"Piece of cake, there's lots of flights from there." Mike smiled. "You can go to your girl's place first if you want…"

"No…"

He turned toward Mize. "She said to come back quickly—I reckon I'll do just that."

"Can't hurt." Mize shrugged. "Get the worst over with a quick as you can. Besides, you do great work in handling impossible jobs." Mike grinned. "It's why my guys attached themselves to you. Come on…" He stood up. "You didn't think it was your rapier wit, did you?" He gave Sean a hug. "Don't worry about it."

"I hope you're right."

"I'm always right."

Sean shook his head and sat down. He scratched his face. *Farrell will know. I'll have to talk to him…*

He looked around. *Once we get back!*

***

The sub, under orders, delivered Sean and his SEAL's to a Naval Base in the Arabian Sea. From there, Sean said goodbye to Mize and his other friends and boarded an aircraft heading to D.C."

His orders told him to get back with 'all speed possible'.

This meant commandeering seats on a cargo plane going in the right direction from a couple of mud marines.

They didn't like it—but Sean did it.

It took two days of travel, but, finally, he found himself, tired but fit, in Andrews Air Force Base.

He found a telephone and, in a shorter time than he had considered possible, was back in the city.

***

"Nice job, kid." Sean was greeted by Farrell, his arm still in a sling. "Glad you didn't have any major problems."

"No," Sean looked toward the corner office. "The Job went like clockwork, my only worry…"

"Was over your order to return with 'all possible speed'," Mary Max appeared, smiling. "We've been talking about you and it was decided…"

Sean looked at her.

"To promote you to 'Special Agent in Charge'"

"Ma'am?"

"We've been talking about it for a bit." She looked at him. "It's been under discussion for some time. There are those higher up that just don't like someone as young as you getting authority." She took a step closer. "I, of course, don't agree with them." She held out a hand. "Congratulations. Whether you know it or not, you deserved it."

"Ma'am, I don't know…"

"Nonsense! You have the tools—the rest will come easily." She took his arm. "Now come inside and tell us everything." She smiled again. "I'm sure it will be quite fascinating…"

He stumbled, then followed along behind Mary Max—it seemed the thing to do.

***

"So that's how I destroyed the Iranian capacity to blow up our ports and hurt vast numbers of people," Sean smiled. "And got promoted in the bargain, although..."

He looked sheepish.

"I'm still not sure I can handle the extra power."

"You can do it." Connie smiled. "You can do most anything!" She looked at him. "I just don't understand how you were able to pull it all off with no one getting hurt."

"None of ours was killed. We had a minor injury of two... But let's talk about you." He smiled. "That is why I got a couple of days off after all.

Connie smiled. "I'm glad." She put her hand on his. "But why don't we take this back to my place—then I'll tell you anything you want to know." She smiled. "Anything at all."

Sean smiled back. Everything was right with his world.

Everything.

THE END

THE END